Los Angeles Stories

GREAT WRITERS ON THE CITY

Los Angeles Stories

GREAT WRITERS ON THE CITY

Edited by John Miller

CHRONICLE BOOKS : SAN FRANCISCO

Printed in the United States of America.

Library of Congress Cataloging in Publication Data

Los Angeles stories : great writers on the city / edited by John
  Miller ; introduction by Eve Babitz.
      p. cm.
    ISBN 0-87701-822-7
    1. Los Angeles (Calif.)–Literary collections.   2. American
literature–California–Los Angeles.   3. American literature–20th
century.   I. Miller, John.
  PS572.L6L6   1991
  813'.01083279494–dc   90-27363
                                                          CIP

Cover image by John Register, *Parking Lot by the Ocean*, 1976.

Distributed in Canada by
Raincoast Books
112 East Third Avenue
Vancouver, B.C. V5T 1C8

10 9 8 7 6 5 4 3 2 1

Chronicle Books
275 Fifth Street
San Francisco, California 94103

For the girl from Palos Verdes

Table of Contents

Introduction

Eve Babitz

W H E N I was seventeen years old I read *Day of the Locust* sitting in my old hammock in our Hollywood backyard, wearing my leopard-skin bathing suit, a Bardot pout on my Sweetheart Pink (by Westmore) lips, my tawny blond hair in a topknot—and I knew just from reading this guy, Nathanael West, that he was probably one of those icky east coast guys with glasses who got mad because when he came to L.A. all those starlets preferred producers or cowboys to him. I mean, Aldous Huxley had written one of those books, too, *Ape and Essence,* only in his, the girl preferred this rich, rich, rich horrible old man to the sensitive and horrified hero. I'd also read *The Loved One*'s send-up of Forest Lawn (which people used to think was a hilarious place) and Edmund Wilson's cracks about how ticky tacky and full of riffraff L.A. was (because it wasn't, alas, New York, and because our tenements weren't like east coast tenements—our poor lived in "shacks" which would have dissolved in one east coast winter but which are still here today since no east coast winter ever came). Early on it had become so fashionable for literary types to find L.A. wanting that no one has ever been able to stop them. Or tried.

I think the attitude of "Well, this place isn't so hot" befell people who came here because of the wholesale carney promoters who just went hog wild in a way that would have been okay for a traveling circus but was a little on the outlandish side for the southern half of a large state. The way Los Angeles made itself sound, it seemed as though people could come here and not be homesick, it was such a paradise. And when people came here and discovered that they were homesick and even sunshine every day couldn't change that, well . . . it seemed a mean, even treacherous trick.

I was born and grew up in L.A. My father came to Boyle Heights when he was sixteen with his Russian Jewish parents who'd escaped from the pogroms and drunken murdering Cossacks back home (so it was hard for them to be homesick). Of course, my poor grandparents were too uneducated and out-of-it to hate L.A. because it wasn't Paris, New York, or London. They just liked waking up with no Cossacks in sunshine every day, and though my grandmother complained a great deal every chance she got, she didn't complain about L.A. L.A. she was grateful for. It was your behavior she thought could use improvement.

My mother was from a small oil town in Texas called Sour Lake. She was twenty-three in 1932 when she left in the middle of the dustbowl depression where the only local heroes were Bonnie and Clyde. She wanted to marry a man in a tuxedo—not a movie star, anyone in a tuxedo. Her first husband was the maitre d' at Ciros and wore a tuxedo every night, but it wasn't until she met my father, the first violinist at the L.A. Philharmonic, that she realized a man in a tuxedo could actually be charismatic, and after a year, she left the first tuxedo and fled to Reno, divorcing the maitre d' to marry my father and live happily ever after. I was born in Hollywood itself in May, just as the jacarandas went into purple blooms (Nabokov's favorite flower and the reason, he once said, he could live in L.A.).

My father's mentor was Igor Stravinsky—they hung around together. Stravinsky was smart, civilized, educated, worldly—a man who realized that if you were going to be anywhere, it might as well be someplace with no war, no snow, and lots of pretty scenery. He moved to Los Angeles for these reasons, plus there were so many adept musicians—studio musicians able to sight-read practically anything, even him. He loved Los Angeles, loved going to Central Avenue where all the jazz musicians played, loved meeting Jelly Roll Morton, loved the mariachi bands, and loved coming to our house on his birthday when my mother would always make him his favorite dish—enchiladas—and Italian rum cake frosted with toasted almonds for dessert.

Whenever I was at the Stravinskys' home when I was growing up, there were always these wonderful Europeans thrilled to be a place with no war and flowers, silken nights filled with night-blooming jasmine. If they thought the place was no good they never complained in print. I got the impression that where they came from must be truly sad, but then, these were the kind of people who knew enough to come in out of the cold and be grateful. Not people like Nathanael West who thought nights weren't everything, who took one look at L.A. and decided that the city was a metaphor for apocalyptic chaos. People who had *really* been in apocalyptic chaos took one look at L.A. and decided that they wanted to go on a picnic.

I think that the kind of people who appreciate L.A. are sensual types, not literary geniuses. Literary types throughout the ages have felt that someone who judges them on criteria of looks and money (L.A.'s basic yardsticks of society), rather than on literary worth, is plainly gross and has no class. If that someone has eccentric and nutty behavior and is *also* a count or a duchess, the literary type in question will probably manage to get along with him (like Evelyn Waugh did). But if the person is bizarre and eccentric and only a vastly wealthy studio head who once made a living selling gloves, then it's not okay for him to be illiterate. Literary types couldn't stand it that Sam Goldwyn should have all that money and power.

Some of the writers herein, particularly West, would have you believe that once people got here "sunshine isn't enough. They get tired of oranges, even of avocado pears and passion fruit." But I have to tell you that my idea of heaven is to live in a hammock swinging between an avocado tree and a lemon tree so I wouldn't have to get up to make guacamole.

But then, sunshine has always been enough for me. For me, the weather, plus the fact that in this century, we've given the world its dreams, beauty, and romance (corny though those dreams may be)— that is enough to make anyone proud. We gave no wars, disasters, or human misery. People who live in Los Angeles really never cared what the rest of the world thought because the minute anyone sensual enough to appreciate picnics comes here, they see for themselves that the cowboys with flat stomachs would naturally get the girls. It was no use sitting around whining about the apocalypse when you could go to the beach or be out hustling a script. The way to have a happy ending in Los Angeles is for the place itself to be enough. It's not New York—but that's the point. In fact, that it's not New York or anyplace else ruthless and cold and brutal *is* the happy ending. No east coast winter ever came. Here we just go on picnics.

F. SCOTT FITZGERALD

Crazy Sunday

IT WAS Sunday—not a day, but rather a gap between two other days. Behind, for all of them, lay sets and sequences, the long waits under the crane that swung the microphone, the hundred miles a day by automobiles to and fro across a county, the struggles of rival ingenuities in the conference rooms, the ceaseless compromise, the clash and strain of many personalities fighting for their lives. And now Sunday, with individual life starting up again, with a glow kindling in eyes that had been glazed with monotony the afternoon before. Slowly as the hours waned they came awake like "Puppenfeen" in a toy shop: an intense colloquy in a corner, lovers disappearing to neck in a hall. And the feeling of "Hurry, it's not too late, but for God's sake hurry before the blessed forty hours of leisure are over."

Joel Coles was writing continuity. He was twenty-eight and not yet broken by Hollywood. He had had what were considered nice assignments since his arrival six months before and he submitted his scenes and sequences with enthusiasm. He referred to himself modestly as a hack but really did not think of it that way. His mother had been a successful actress; Joel had spent his childhood between London and New York trying to separate the real from the unreal, or at least to keep one guess ahead. He was a handsome man with the pleasant cow-brown eyes that in 1913 had gazed out at Broadway audiences from his mother's face.

When the invitation came it made him sure that he was getting somewhere. Ordinarily he did not go out on Sundays but stayed sober and took work home with him. Recently they had given him a Eugene O'Neill play destined for a very important lady indeed. Everything he had done so far had pleased Miles Calman, and Miles Calman was the only director on the lot who did not work under a supervisor and was responsible to the money men alone. Everything was clicking into place in Joel's career. ("This is Mr. Calman's secretary. Will you come to tea from four to six Sunday—he lives in Beverly Hills, number—.")

Joel was flattered. It would be a party out of the top-drawer. It was a tribute to himself as a young man of promise. The Marion Davies crowd, the high-hats, the big currency numbers, perhaps even Dietrich and Garbo and the Marquise, people who were not seen everywhere, would probably be at Calman's.

"I won't take anything to drink," he assured himself. Calman was audibly tired of rummies, and thought it was a pity the industry could not get along without them.

Joel agreed that writers drank too much—he did himself, but he wouldn't this afternoon. He wished Miles would be within hearing when the cocktails were passed to hear his succinct, unobtrusive, "No, thank you."

Miles Calman's house was built for great emotional moments—there was an air of listening, as if the far silences of its vistas hid an audience, but this afternoon it was thronged, as though people had been bidden rather than asked. Joel noted with pride that only two other writers from the studio were in the crowd, an ennobled limey and, somewhat to his surprise, Nat Keogh, who had evoked Calman's impatient comment on drunks.

Stella Calman (Stella Walker, of course) did not move on to her other guests after she spoke to Joel. She lingered—she looked at him with the sort of beautiful look that demands some sort of acknowledgment and Joel drew quickly on the dramatic adequacy inherited from his mother:

"Well, you look about sixteen! Where's your kiddy car?"

She was visibly pleased; she lingered. He felt that he should say something more, something confident and easy—he had first met her when she was struggling for bit in New York. At the moment a tray slid up and Stella put a cocktail glass into his hand.

"Everybody's afraid, aren't they?" he said, looking at it absently. "Everybody watches for everybody else's blunders, or tries to make sure they're with people that'll do them credit. Of course that's not true in your house," he covered himself hastily. "I just meant generally in Hollywood."

Stella agreed. She presented several people to Joel as if he were very important. Reassuring himself that Miles was at the other side of the room, Joel drank the cocktail.

"So you have a baby?" he said. "That's the time to look out. After a pretty woman has had her first child, she's very vulnerable, because she wants to be reassured about her own charm. She's got to have some new man's unqualified devotion to prove to herself she hasn't lost anything."

"I never get anybody's unqualified devotion," Stella said rather resentfully.

"They're afraid of your husband."

"You think that's it?" She wrinkled her brow over the idea; then the conversation was interrupted at the exact moment Joel would have chosen.

Her attentions had given him confidence. Not for him to join safe groups, to slink to refuge under the wings of such acquaintances as he saw about the room. He walked to the window and looked out toward the Pacific, colorless under its sluggish sunset. It was good here—the American Riviera and all that, if there were ever time to enjoy it. The handsome, well-dressed people in the room, the lovely girls, and the—well, the lovely girls. You couldn't have everything.

He saw Stella's fresh boyish face, with the tired eyelid that always drooped a little over one eye, moving about among her guests and he wanted to sit with her and talk a long time as if she were a girl instead of a name; he followed her to see if she paid anyone as much attention as she had paid him. He took another cocktail—not because he needed confidence but because she had given him so much of it. Then he sat down beside the director's mother.

"Your son's gotten to be a legend, Mrs. Calman—Oracle and a Man of Destiny and all that. Personally, I'm against him but I'm in a minority. What do you think of him? Are you impressed? Are you surprised how far he's gone?"

"No, I'm not surprised," she said calmly. "We always expected a lot from Miles."

"Well now, that's unusual," remarked Joel. "I always think all mothers are like Napoleon's mother. My mother didn't want me to have anything to do with the entertainment business. She wanted me to go to West Point and be safe."

"We always had every confidence in Miles." . . .

He stood by the built-in bar of the dining room with the good-humored, heavy-drinking, highly paid Nat Keogh.

"—I made a hundred grand during the year and lost forty grand gambling, so now I've hired a manager."

"You mean an agent," suggested Joel.

"No, I've got that too. I mean a manager. I make over everything to my wife and then he and my wife get together and hand me out the money. I pay him five thousand a year to hand me out my money."

"You mean your agent."

"No, I mean my manager, and I'm not the only one—a lot of other irresponsible people have him."

"Well, if you're irresponsible why are you responsible enough to hire a manager?"

"I'm just irresponsible about gambling. Look here—"

A singer performed; Joel and Nat went forward with the others to listen.

The singing reached Joel vaguely; he felt happy and friendly toward all the people gathered there, people of bravery and industry, superior to a bourgeoisie that outdid them in ignorance and loose living, risen to a position of the highest prominence in a nation that for a decade had wanted only to be entertained. He liked them—he loved them. Great waves of good feeling flowed through him.

As the singer finished his number and there was a drift toward the hostess to say good-by, Joel had an idea. He would give them "Building It Up," his own composition. It was his only parlor trick, it had amused several parties and it might please Stella Walker. Possessed by the hunch, his blood throbbing with the scarlet corpuscles of exhibitionism, he sought her.

"Of course," she cried. "Please! Do you need anything?"

"Someone has to be the secretary that I'm supposed to be dictating to."

"I'll be her."

As the word spread, the guests in the hall, already putting on their coats to leave, drifted back and Joel faced the eyes of many strangers. He had a dim foreboding, realizing that the man who had just performed was a famous radio entertainer. Then someone said "Sh!" and he was alone with Stella, the center of a sinister Indian-like half-circle. Stella smiled up at him expectantly—he began.

His burlesque was based upon the cultural limitations of Mr. Dave Silverstein, an independent producer; Silverstein was presumed to be dictating a letter outlining a treatment of a story he had bought.

"—a story of divorce, the younger generators and the Foreign Legion," he heard his voice saying, with the intonations of Mr. Silverstein. "But we got to build it up, see?"

Λ sharp pang of doubt struck through him. The faces surrounding him in the gently molded light were intent and curious, but there was no ghost of a smile anywhere; directly in front the Great Lover of the screen glared at him with an eye as keen as the eye of a potato. Only Stella Walker looked up at him with a radiant, never faltering smile.

"If we make him a Menjou type, then we get a sort of Michael Arlen only with a Honolulu atmosphere."

Still not a ripple in front, but in the rear a rustling, a perceptible shift toward the left, toward the front door.

"—then she says she feels this sex appil for him and he burns out and says 'Oh, go on destroy yourself—'"

At some point he heard Nat Keogh snicker and here and there were a few encouraging faces, but as he finished he had the sickening realization that he had made a fool of himself in view of an important section of the picture world, upon whose favor depended his career.

For a moment he existed in the midst of a confused silence, broken by a general trek for the door. He felt the undercurrent of derision that rolled through the gossip; then—all this was in the space of ten seconds—the Great Lover, his eye hard and empty as the eye of a needle, shouted "Boo! Boo!" voicing in an overtone what he felt was the mood of the crowd. It was the resentment of the professional toward the amateur, of the community toward the stranger, the thumbs-down of the clan.

Only Stella Walker was still standing near and thanking him as if he had been an unparalleled success, as if it hadn't occurred to her that anyone hadn't liked it. As Nat Keogh helped him into his overcoat, a great wave of self-disgust swept over him and he clung desperately to his rule of never betraying an inferior emotion until he no longer felt it.

"I was a flop," he said lightly to Stella. "Never mind, it's a good number when appreciated. Thanks for your coöperation."

The smile did not leave her face—he bowed rather drunkenly and Nat drew him toward the door. . . .

The arrival of his breakfast awakened him into a broken and ruined world. Yesterday he was himself, a point of fire against an industry, today he felt that he was pitted under an enormous disadvantage, against those faces, against individual contempt and collective sneer. Worse than that, to Miles Calman he was become one of those rummies, stripped of dignity, whom Calman regretted he was compelled to use. To Stella Walker on whom he had forced a martyrdom to preserve the courtesy of her house—her opinion he did not dare to guess. His gastric juices ceased to flow and he set his poached eggs back on the telephone table. He wrote:

"Dear Miles: You can imagine my profound self-disgust. I confess to a taint of exhibitionism, but at six o'clock in the afternoon, in broad daylight! Good God! My apologies to your wife.

"Yours ever,
"Joel Coles."

Joel emerged from his office on the lot only to slink like a malefactor to the tobacco store. So suspicious was his manner that one of the studio police asked to see his admission card. He had decided to eat lunch outside when Nat Keogh, confident and cheerful, overtook him.

"What do you mean you're in permanent retirement? What if that Three-Piece Suit did boo you?

"Why, listen," he continued, drawing Joel into the studio restaurant. "The night of one of his premières at Grauman's, Joe Squires kicked his tail while he was bowing to the crowd. The ham said Joe'd hear from him later but when Joe called him up at eight o'clock next day and said, 'I thought I was going to hear from you,' he hung up the phone."

The preposterous story cheered Joel, and he found a gloomy consolation in staring at the group at the next table, the sad, lovely

Siamese twins, the mean dwarfs, the proud giant from the circus picture. But looking beyond at the yellow-stained faces of pretty women, their eyes all melancholy and startling with mascara, their ball gowns garish in full day, he saw a group who had been at Calman's and winced.

"Never again," he exclaimed aloud, "absolutely my last social appearance in Hollywood!"

The following morning a telegram was waiting for him at his office:

"You were one of the most agreeable people at our party. Expect you at my sister June's buffet supper next Sunday.

"Stella Walker Calman."

The blood rushed fast through his veins for a feverish minute. Incredulously he read the telegram over.

"Well, that's the sweetest thing I ever heard of in my life!"

1940

KATE BRAVERMAN

Palm Latitudes

A S F R A N C I S C A studies the boulevard, she decides
that she does not dislike this City of the Angels, with its alleys of
bougainvillea, with its insistent yellow and bright-orange canna
studding narrow paths between bungalow-walled courts where only
blood relatives dare walk. Now this collection of angels and asphalt,
of stunted shrubbery and bamboo-fenced alleys dense with magenta
crepe bougainvillea calls itself Los Angeles. She shrugs, feeling the
wounded density of the city settling across her skin. It is a geography
with themes that are recurrent like the bands of color in weavings. It
is a specific design she had learned to navigate and survive.

There are no surprises in this particular fabric, with the packs of
dogs and barefoot children with black hair and black almond eyes. She
barely notices when they call her puta and toss bits of gravel near her.
They are careful. No rock has ever grazed her flesh. She is an object
of curiosity and fear. She is what glows in the night, the eye that does
not sleep. She might be a sort of religious symbol. She leans against the
wooden bus bench, reassured by the nearby garages and restaurants
painted an aggressive yellow or red. The assertion of primary color is
fundamental to the fibers of this weaving. It is lulling, like sleeping
beside an ocean.

From her bus bench, she can see the orange-tiled roofs of
Spanish-style houses planted in the sides of hills like a series of terra-
cotta pots, almost ornamental. From a certain angle, this area could
be Mexico City or Santa Clara, Caracas or San Juan. The pattern
repeats itself like an insane weaver or a cancer, even in this southern
city which seems only peripherally and accidentally American.
This city which was once an outpost of Spain and once a region of
Mexico. This city webbed with boulevards bearing the names of
Spanish psychotics and saints. This incomplete city which seems to

have no recognizable past, no ground that could be called unassailably sacred. This incomplete city that speaks of an impending terror.

It occurs to her that what she most appreciates about this City of the Angels is that which is missing, the voids, the unstitched borders, the empty corridors, the not yet deciphered. She is grateful for the absence of history and its physical manifestations, the granite cathedrals of the imported God, the wide tiled plazas and the assault of church bells, the church bells that scarred her later, in Mexico City, with Ramón.

It was a Sunday. Church bells were screeching everywhere, maniacally, like legions of lunatics or birds, millions of trapped and enraged jungle birds scratching at the air. Ramón was giving her twelve thousand American dollars. He was pressing an airplane ticket into her hands. But her fingers would not open. She held an invisible silk fan in her hands, pearls, a bouquet of orchids, white as a wedding gown. She was his concubine. They were of the same substance, indivisible. In time, he would shed his too-thin American wife, that woman of granite and angles. She was an aberration that did not belong, like cathedrals in the jungle. He would banish that bleached white bitch and marry her. There was no other possible resolution.

And she did not understand what Ramón was saying. The car was moving and she noticed only that her suitcases were packed, not his. Bells were ringing everywhere, birds were flying in sharp formations, frenzied, with no place to perch. The spires were poisoned with danger and clanging. The stones were a contagion. The sky crowded with low-flying demented flocks of shrieking birds, and something had gone wrong with her ears.

"What are these?" she asked in English. Ramón always insisted they speak in English. Even in her panic, she did not violate their ritual. "What are these?" she repeated. She was pointing to her suitcases.

"They are your bags, obviously. They are packed. We are driving to the airport. You are leaving," Ramón informed her. But she was deaf. She was reading his lips.

Yesterday, they had toured the museum. She had studied the feathered capes of Aztec lords, intricate and stunning with the green-and-purple plumage of long-extinct birds. She had seen the great round stones which measured time with an accuracy and precision mathematics could not begin to imagine. She understood the civilization on display before her. The Aztec Empire erected pyramids without the wheel. The implications of magic were irrefutable. She had experienced a grandeur and a majestic heat old and holy. And Ramón was a lord. He should wear the skin of jaguars and sandals of snakeskin.

They embraced in front of the Aztec clock and she was naked, air to air with everyone, dead and alive, real and imagined. They were beyond bodies. Time split, cross-sectioned. Borders were erased as simply as lines of chalk on a sidewalk during a storm.

This was the culture the Spaniards had destroyed. They had gutted the temples, burned holy books, artifacts, the magic and plumes. A band of exiled syphilitic renegades had pronounced this civilization as savage. And the priests had blessed them in this. Ramón wrapped her in his arms as she stood in the museum and wept.

Then the enormities were defined. There were steps down to the core of the earth. The path was captioned and mapped. She knew exactly who she was. Her fingers were flowers, flames. She owned the wind, the seasons, the paths of stars and the artifacts of all women and men. Now Ramón was speaking and she could not hear him.

"I have refined your sensibility, given you an outline of art and history, a vocabulary and reference points in two languages. The world is divided into women who ride buses and women who hail cabs. You know who you are. You will survive."

Then Ramón was giving her the box he had purchased for her in London and kept hidden in his office safe. He was handing her the marble box lined with black velvet. Within the box were the silver and gold bracelets which were also kept locked in his office. She was wearing the ruby ring. Ramón was placing small square pieces of paper in her uncomprehending hands and explaining the intricacies of bearer bonds. He was her patrón. She was being dismissed.

But she could understand nothing. The air had dissolved into a sharp and formless static. Deaf and mute, she kept pointing to the back seat, to her suitcases. They glared at her like a deformity, like a leper in the cobblestone-stained alleys of certain almost deserted ports, a leper begging without hands for dimes.

"They are Louis Vuitton," Ramón said. He seemed simultaneously sad and frantic, partly because of her, she realized, and partly because of the suitcases. "They are the only Louis Vuitton bags you will ever own. Try to hang on to them."

Hang on to them? She stared at him through her French sunglasses. Did he think she was mad, that she would lose her suitcases or simply throw them away? Did he think she did not yet understand how to travel, how to present a claim check, nod with one finger to summon a porter, a taxi, a concierge? Did she not often return from their trips alone, to prepare the house for La Señora, to be there as if she had not moved farther than the patio since La Señora left?

A dark-blue car stops. Francisca slides in. It is a short drive around the park with the grayish lake of water weeds and ducks, two blocks precisely. She glances at the ruined Los Angeles sky and realizes it is better this way, cloudless, bells silent, without the hypocrisy of rituals that have been too long obsolete. It is less offensive to forget entirely than to remember incorrectly, defectively. And Ramón was saying, You must go, this afternoon, now. I am falling in love with you. But, she was saying, but, she was saying, but, like a record struck, but what on earth do you mean?

Francisca leads the man up the stairs to her apartment. Across the narrow hallway, a Mexicano couple turn their radio louder and casually, with elaborate grace, close their door without once looking directly at her. The white man behind her has light hair turning gray at the edges like an upkept plot of land surrendering to dead weeds.

La Puta de la Luna eases herself out of her skirt. She lets the silk drift to the floor like petals from a flower. Then she erases the man with the weeds at his temple from her consciousness, thinks instead of her sister Delfina's last letter, now three months unanswered. She must respond immediately. Delfina said the government finally restored the power plant. For three days there were radios and phonographs, lights that blazed, fiestas and dancing. Then los guerrilleros bombed the power plant again. She must express her regrets.

There is a man above her, gray like a cloud or smoke. He has no weight. He is merely the illusion of space. And Delfina wrote, "You tell us nothing of your new patrón or the nature of his family."

Delfina, whose firstborn son died of pneumonia the previous winter. And she must remember to express her regret that the son of her father's cousin, Alberto Gómez, she can almost remember him, was killed fighting in the hills near the capital. Once she had been diligent with her communications. Once she had sent cards embossed with candles and birds and flowers. Now she can no longer bear addressing a card to the village of her birth. It seems an act of subterfuge, a form of impossibility, like communicating with the dead or attempting to telephone someone you have encountered only in dreams.

The American man is quick and clean, wanting almost nothing. Pale bastard, she thinks, afraid to drop your pants in dark alleys. Or to tear the sheet with your teeth when you come, like a woman giving birth, in pain and exhilaration. White erased thing, you cannot even imagine boarding a strange train that has no destination, a vehicle where they ask not for dollars but for your mouth.

Her contempt for the man passes. She is particularly grateful he does not speak. Americans crave the exotic, but they are streamlined like their highways, gray as the asphalt they invent to surround them. Their desires are predictable, run in cycles, like fashions. They do not know that the sea could wash them like paint.

She glances at the graying man, who is lighting a cigarette, already impatient, reclothing himself with rapidity, ashes fall upon the sleeve of his dark-blue jacket. He has the look of a man who realizes he has made not a terrible mistake, but rather an avoidable miscalculation. A man who drank an extra martini and missed an airplane, perhaps.

La Puta de la Luna is fastening her skin of burgundy. The man is hurrying and silent. She encourages him to remain mute. Yes, American men are clean and simple. The most offensive aspect of American men is their relentless desire to talk. They lack the facility for intuition, even in a primitive form. Such impulses have been removed from them. They do not understand it is all an ebb and flow, a shearing and an adornment, a ceaseless flowing where nothing is permanent. Their sky has been sealed, welded shut, tight as a coffin. The relation of stars to the side of a hill, the purpose of the winds and migrating birds, are phenomena they can no longer imagine.

Of course Americans are severed from their earth connections. The flesh exists only as a metaphor for them, a symbol. They have no sense of boundaries, as if the entire world were one concrete parking lot. They violate her integrity with their questions, their assumptions, their compulsion to identify. They want her history, bare and naked. They want not just her body, which is easy, but her secrets. When they speak to her, they sound as if they were all writing books or working for La Migra or planning to start a church.

Young men who cannot afford her describe their occupations and anxieties, as if she could provide them with answers, definitions, absolution. The young men who cannot afford her reveal hidden fears, admit that the towers and Municipal Court buildings sicken them. At night, alone, they write movie scripts no one wishes to purchase. They look at her as if she were a curandera, a gitana. It is as if they expect her to sing for them, to decipher lost tongues, dance with veils, read the tarot, decode their dreams and draw maps of their destiny. The flesh is not enough. It is abstractions, pyramids of words they crave.

After the perfunctory caress, passionless, with their hands like leafless whittled braches, they stare at her, longing for more. She stares back through eyes painted with the flawless blues of long-extinct birds. She can outwait them. Any woman could.

Women have waited millions of years, growing separate as another species, with visions and priorities no man-words, no man-measurements can comprehend. Women spark dark cracks in the wanton night. Women exist in isolated unfathomable perfection, creatures of nuance and implication. Women are like aberrant stars, suddenly changing orbits. Or an unconforming sea, resisting the obvious structures of piers and harbors, refusing to be merely blue or green, tame as a formula. It is women who shift the borders. The seasons run wild. Women flow and slide. Men are larger. Women eat the silence. Women survive.

The man with the graying hair and nicotine smell staining the skin of his fingers is quiet in the car. His silence comes not from respect, she realizes, but rather from an internal preoccupation. He switches on the car radio. It is the news in English. The terrible heat wave that set the mountains ablaze, poisoned the air and closed the downtown factories has abated. The night will be cooler. And they sit, unconnected, at a traffic light.

Francisca exits the car and walks slowly back to her bus bench. She glances at the park behind her. The aged woman is still sitting at the edge of the lake, staring into the shadow-dented water as if it were a page of a book that she could read. And it is possible this old woman has mastered the art of deciphering the fluid nuances of water and shadow, the intervals of silence and what they imply.

Tonight, the moon will be full. Francisca is suddenly aware that the ancient woman is also thinking about the moon and its impending fullness, how it has once again completed its journey into the round and temporary whole. Women turn on a lunar cycle. It is not mathematics or equations but the pull of the moon which makes them bleed. It is men who seek to chart space. Women already know that space is inhabited. Each month, women feel eggs and stars and infant unborn moons dies and squeeze through their wounded wombs.

Francisca cannot erase the presence of the old woman on the shore of the lake. Somehow, this woman seems familiar. But no, she cannot possibly know this aged mestiza who is studying the surface of the lake as if decoding hieroglyphics. Francisca knows no one in this city. Yet there is a sense of recognition between them. She admires the old woman's patience, her graceful surrendering to mere waiting. This particular aged woman knows that the world is composed of rented rooms where women in faded half-slips sip sherry and pills. Their shoes strap at the ankle. They soak their feet in salted basins. Their painted toenails are chipped. The body is going to ruin like an insignificant and deserted port the jungle has begun to swallow.

In Madrid or Caracas or Los Angeles, it is the same indifferent neon, a radio, a phone call which does or does not come. There is a bouquet of carnations or roses two days past dead. You pretend that someone sent them, that you did not buy them yourself. This small subterfuge infuses the decaying petals with a dignity, a significance. Always, there are the trivial details, the tiny invented anchors designed to keep the waters from flooding in. A standard-issue bird in a cage or a standard-issue cat to be fed. The plants in terra-cotta pots to water. The button or hem to sew. The sun goes down and it is all less than you ever planned.

La Puta de la Luna stares into the passing traffic. She thinks of the card she must write to her sister. Delfina knows nothing of Ramón or the airplane which carried her, deaf and mute, from Mexico City to San Juan. Or how, after being mistress to a patrón, she could no longer keep her place, her pose of subservience, her falsely cemented lips. The rocks and pebbles had been spit from her mouth. Her fraudulence, her pose of ignorance, it was a thing she shed simply, naturally, as one tosses off an old coat.

And the first American family in Miami, with their sandy-haired blue-eyed boy-children, called her arrogant and sullen. She understood their English perfectly and more, what their words implied. They demanded the illusion of gulfs and uncrossable rivers. It was intrinsic to their functioning that she be perceived as different, as a thing with distinct and recognizable borders. She must be like a miniature country in the jungle mountains that one squadron of American airplanes could entirely destroy between breakfast and lunch. This is the design they understand, the configuration they insist be repeated in the exterior geography of nations and in the internal geography of people.

But she had sailed that particular gulf, had navigated and mastered that current. She could no longer merely pretend to be a lamp, a toaster, an oven waiting for their white mouths to order her off or on. It was the tone, Francisca now realizes, the same staccato precision that might be used to order the decimation of the farmlands of a small and insignificant nation. A region inhabited by women and men with brown or yellow-tinged skin.

She longs to explain to Delfina that she has learned certain intricacies of the body which are not a transgression but a blessing, a removal of self-imposed infirmities. Is it a sin for a woman who has been crippled to walk without a cane?

Once, she felt desire in the slow warming morning while Ramón slept and she waited for him to wake, in Caracas or Mexico City, in Puerto Vallarta or Managua, or in Santa Clara in the West Indian islands where the patrón and his wife had their second home. Santa Clara on the Caribbean, the youngest of God's oceans, the still green sea. There she waited for Ramón silent as clay, open to the bone, stripped as a bride at dawn on her wedding day, beyond breathless and becalmed.

She brushed her long black hair and thought, I was born to love you. It is my destiny, what I outwitted a starved and aborted girlhood for, entire sections of me intact, vast and unused like an uncharted continent or an absolute vow.

As she watched Ramón sleeping, she thought, I am every woman whose flower-print sheets you ever lay on. I am every woman wearing white silk slips and French perfume, bending above plants on terraces and balconies in whichever country or sunset. It was my lips that promised to love you forever, that moaned Siempre, por vida, oh baby. It is my face lingering unique and fragrant in your corridors, in the hollows anchoring your bones, in the blood canals where birds thought to be extinct call in your sleeping aviaries, eating the darkness with their mouths.

After Ramón she could no longer lie in a back room shared with a child, where a door might be opened without warning at any instant, a lamp switched on. She no longer slept easily, like an appliance turned off, like a candle blown out. Now she took sleeping tablets from the medicine cabinets and jewelry boxes of the patrón and La Señora. She drank their liquor.

Now she touched her body in the darkness and made herself shudder, sinning both in the act and in the remembering. And she has said to Ramón, Take me, my dreams of fish and rain forests, all that is lavish and green. I give you my skin to paint. Tattoo your name on my thigh. Christen me with your hands and tongue. Love me as if I were pulled from your loins, as if I had nested months in your belly, your chest, and exploded your groin with my birth.

Sometimes, in the night, in the room of a stranger, she would remember specific incidents with a clarity that amazed her. She sat with Ramón on a restaurant terrace in Puerto Vallarta. They drank rum from the shells of coconuts. Men in red-and-white parachutes dropped from the undamaged fields of blue sky. The breeze took them like red-and-white petals. The waters were warm, calm, adorned with small black sharks. Ramón had glared at the American tourist at a nearby table and said, "If you look at my woman's leg again I will kill you." She remembered Ramón's words, parted her legs and with her fingers made herself feel thunder.

Now Francisca paces the pavement bordering the acre of city

park, restless and agitated, surprised that the images still burn. And in the park the palms are beginning their hopeless surrender to the dusk, to the night that will be luminescent beyond expectation, brilliant and devious, more an equation than a lullaby and, as always, absolutely empty. This is a configuration which cannot be resolved.

La Puta de la Luna tosses her cigarette into the gutter. Perhaps she will answer Delfina's letter tomorrow. She will invent conventional lies. She will not attempt to describe what it is to be swallowed by a borderless other. It came to her with an urgency she could not deny or resist. And it was not an act of innocence.

On the other side of the illusionary waters she discovered she was subtly altered. She allowed herself to merge with a certain slice of city view, a particular collection of angles and shadows, spires and the green glaze settling across a terrace of philodendrons in terra-cotta pots. At such moments, her fingers stopped polishing the silver tray the family rarely used. She would abandon her assigned task and stand in a sunlit study instead.

Of course, the flesh had its own life, she recognized. The pulse was natural, was a river carving its own channel, employing temporary human vessels. And she realized that rooms and walls were transitory illusions, symbolic, meaningless without the consent of shared context. And she could no longer consent.

Her body seemed to shrink and swell. She stumbled into morning, blinded. It occurred to her that sometimes women turn to their secret, sexual side. Men were different. They were born with the sun on their bellies. They had absolute direction from inception. Women were daughters of the moon, with circular seasons, with one portion of themselves exposed and the other perpetually hidden and dark.

Then there was a second American family, a third and a fourth. And the next family called her lazy. La Señora suspected she was ill and suggested she consult a doctor.

Francisca remembers this and smiles. There is no doctor for her, no curandera, no prescription or herb potion, however exotic or difficult to gather and combine. There are no vaccinations for her disease, no Hail Marys, incantations or amulets, no composition of elements which fortune or imagination can invent. She has merged with the virus, the infection, the delirium that invaded her. They are one. She cannot be saved by candles lit in cathedrals or a visit to a sanitarium or a distant and indisputably hallowed shrine, not even a house where a saint was born and a certified miracle performed.

1988

OSCAR ZETA ACOSTA

The Revolt of the Cockroach People

WHITTIER BOULEVARD – The Strip. Saturday morning. Mexican restaurants, Adelita's, La Iguana de Oro, The Latin Strip, dime stores, pawn shops, radio and television repair, finance companies, Woolworth's, J. C. Penney, Sears, Jack-In-The-Box, McDonald's, Department of Social Welfare, Hollenbeck Police Station. We cross Atlantic, Olympic, Indiana, Brooklyn, Soto. . . . Thousands of faces, posters colored red and green, banners of Brown Eagles, the Azteca black and white and red Thunderbird, LA HUELGA, LUCHA, MAPA, LULAC, BROWN BERETS, CON SAFOS, LA RAZA, COPA, CHICANO LIBERATION FRONT, CMO, MECHA, MALDEF, ACLU, NATIONAL LAWYERS GUILD, CHICANO LAW STUDENTS, EICC, EL TEATRO CAMPESINO, CHICANO DANCE GROUP DE UCLA, SOCO Y ZETA FOREVER, ROSE CHERNIN, DOROTHY HEALEY, NEIL HERRING, FACES OF BROWN, FACES OF LONG HAIR, BOOTS, MARCHING, FISTS SWING, VATOS LOCOS PINTOS CHICANOS HIPPIES COCKROACHES BOOT SHOE HEEL TOE TRAMP TRAMP TRAMP. . . .

We are looking at a color film of the Chicano Moratorium of August 29, 1970.

Suddenly, Laguna Park. Two square blocks. Flat green. Enclosed by wire fence and line of tall palm trees. I see a swimming pool, a gymnasium and a sandbox with swings and a merry-go-round of iron bars. Thousands of people mill around, sitting on the green grass with children, eating hot dogs, tortillas, soda pop, singing, smoking, smiling, pretty girls, young dudes a little drunk, falling, jumping, horsing around, a picnic, a Saturday afternoon in the park, groups of bearded men, strong men in brown khaki, in brown brogans. A peaceful gentle scene.

The film cuts to a ballfield in the center of the park. A wooden stage is at home plate. The camera is on the pitcher's mound.

Short dark girl of Aztlan in dress of white, ruffled in orange and red, little flowers and red-orange ribbons in her black hair: the flamenco dancer from UCLA. She dances with some kid—buck teeth, slick legs in tight cowboy pants, sombrero in hand, boots clicking at the hard floor, black hair falling over his joker face, a two-step *ranchera*.

SLASH! The film is cut to a liquor store on Whittier Boulevard, at the corner of Indiana, two blocks from the park. The camera is hand-carried and the picture bounces. It moves us toward the front of the liquor store. The sun is reflected off the lens, a streak of yellow. LAGUNA LIQUORS in black letters on plate glass; a grill of black iron bars covers it all. Inside the store, if you look close, you can see people staring through the glass into the street. These people have hands to eyes, to mouths, they are calling out to other people on the street. On the sidewalk outside the store, you see the line of helmeted pigs in leather jackets, in brown suits, in white helmets, in battle gear, with huge guns in hand, with rifles, bazookas, with tear gas equipment. You see them close up, the faces of armed men staring into the liquor store.

And now you see people suddenly coming out. Now you see a cop lunge for a kid with long black hair.

Cut to the sidewalk.

A kid is swinging at a cop. He has a red headband. The cops are pushing the people on the sidewalk. The people are being struck with the clubs.

The camera jerks. Shot to the sidewalk cement, shot up to the body of a fat cop, camera is moving along the ground and now you see a line of uniformed cops in helmets lining the middle of the street, batons in hand at parade rest. Across the street you see a crowd of people, mostly kids, leaning back, standing staunchly, some with hands on hips, stretched out wide, feet apart, hands up in the air, yelling, shouting; but no sound on this film. You cannot hear anything but the buzz of the reel in the back of the darkened courtroom that is singularly silent now as you tense and feel strains of goose bumps in your hair because you see on film, a *real* document, not from the movies, not TV, you know it really happened, you have seen the burnt streets, you have walked them, you recognize some of the faces, some of the stores, you know exactly where the corners of Indiana and Whittier are, you have driven across that intersection a hundred times, you have eaten menudo at the restaurant on the corner, you've eaten burritos at the hot dog stand across from the park, you have been in that park yourself. . . .

I remember a winter day in 1969 when I marched with some five thousand along the same route, in the rain. We took to the streets without any fanfare. And by the time we reached Laguna Park, with rain and thunder and lightning and ice-cold wind at our faces, the crowd started to disperse. It wanted no speeches. It wanted warmth and comfort.

I remember jumping up on a park bench and grabbing a bullhorn and telling the people to return, to listen to the voices of thunder and lightning: we may be the last generation of Chicanos if we don't stop the war. If we don't stop the destruction of our culture, we may not be around for the next century. We are the Viet Cong of America. Tooner Flats is Mylai. Just because Peaches and Reddin haven't started throwing napalm doesn't mean they have stopped the war. The Poverty Program of Johnson, the Welfare of Roosevelt, Truman, Eisenhower and Kennedy, The New Deal and The Old Deal, The New Frontier as well as Nixon's American Revolution . . . these are further embellishments of the government's pacification program.

Therefore, there is only one issue: LAND. We need to get our own land. We need our own government. We must have our own flag and our own country. Nothing less will save the existence of the Chicanos.

And I let it go at that.

I did not tell them how to implement the deal.

I did not, nor did any other speaker, tell them to take up arms prior to August 29, 1970.

Again the film shows us the park, a distortion of what we saw just a few minutes ago. Then there was order and laughter. Now there is chaos: legs, arms, hair in wind, running kids, people in scrambling motions, running away from the camera, away from the cops advancing in platoon formation, a phalanx of pigs, guns, smoke, bottles in air, clubs swinging; until the formation breaks up, pigs mix with the kids in T shirts, without shirts, barefooted teenagers, mostly boys, young men, but some *cholas,* some broads with bottles in hand. They clash in the middle of the field.

SLASH!

Whittier Boulevard is burning. Tooner Flats is going up in flames. Smoke, huge columns of black smoke looming over the buildings. Telephone wires dangling loose from the poles. Everywhere the pavement is covered with broken bottles and window glass. Mannequins from Leed's Clothing lie about like war dead. Somehow a head from a wig shop is rolling eerily down the road. Here a police van overturned, its engine smoking. There a cop car, flames shooting out the windows. Cops marching forward with gas masks down the middle of the debris. An ordinary day in Saigon, Haiphong, Quang Tri and Tooner Flats.

DARKNESS.

Then the overhead lights come on, the bailiff opens the shades. Daytime in the courtroom: The State vs. The Tooner Flats Seven, charged with Arson, Riot, Conspiracy and a host of other travesties.

Torrez steps forward to the witness stand. He is a lean dark-brown Chicano, prosecuting the biggest case of his career. He has on one of his typical silk suits from Macy's. Younger, the DA, appointed him specially for this trial. Chicano defendants and defense attorney and prosecution. And there on the bench is good old Chicano lackey, Superior Court Judge Alfred Alacran. Alacran cuts a fine figure: soft gray temples, black hornrimmed glasses. An exact man who moves with deliberation. He smiles often, but not at me. *Me,* he hates. He smiles and always looks as if he just came back from Mazatlan in a Jaguar with a tall blonde. And if he were not a pig and a flunky, he would probably have been the most famous Chicano lawyer in the history of East LA.

Torrez is speaking to the witness, Peter Peaches, the man who beat me out for Sheriff.

"Now, Sheriff Peaches," Torrez says, "we have seen the film your department prepared. But could you please explain to the jury in your own words what happened after the Chicanos left Laguna Park."

Peter Peaches is smiling. Why not, when he can watch a bunch of brown pawns tear one another apart, slave against slave? He wears his khaki uniform, his military cap in his lap.

"To be blunt, all hell broke loose."

"What happened?"

He frowns, pretending to struggle with his memory. "They sent some of their men into Laguna Liquors."

I am on my feet. "Objection. . . . Vague and hearsay."

"Overruled," Alacran barks. "Proceed."

"Tell us, Sheriff," Torrez says, "where you got your information."

"We sent in our undercover man, Officer Fernando Sumaya. He has all the firsthand information you want."

"Thank you for coming down, Sheriff," Alacran says. "I believe you're excused for now." Urbanely, he consults his watch. "After noon recess, call Officer Sumaya to the stand." He rises, the courtroom heaves up. We are adjourned for lunch.

Immediately I am surrounded by my clients, asking me for the umpteenth time how it is going. Rodolfo Corky Gonzales, Gilbert Rodriguez, Jose Ramirez and Raul Raza of *La Voz*, both short tough hardnosed militants; then Waterbuffalo and Bullwinkle from the CMs, two monstrous anarchists from Aztlanvilla; and lastly my new Miss *Esa*, Elena Lowrider, a tough broad with a big hot body. We all make a lot of noise and the court reporter who is tidying up, the blonde bitch Mrs. Wilson, glares at me from behind the stand with the microphone which I use. Or which I am supposed to use, according to Alacran who had held me in contempt a dozen times since this gig began six months ago or whenever.

But I am a man with a million things on his mind and sometimes I forget to use it, forget to show proper respect and this too offends him. I have manners, but I simply forget about them when I'm with guys like Gilbert or Pelon or Sailor Boy, the little kid who came up to me a few months ago and said he was supposed to be one of my bodyguards. He'd been in prison since he was a teenager, in and out for drugs and then one death.

"I get me one *muerte, ese*," he told me then. "So if I go back again, this time they ain't gonna cut me loose." Somebody had kicked his brother's head until the brother went blind, so Sailor Boy stuck a blade into the dude's heart. They stuck Sailor Boy into a Federal joint:

"And that's where I turned on to *acido, ese* . . . These dudes gave me some of that Blue, you know? I was just sitting in my cell alone. I hardly never went out. I just sat and read. We had all the *carga* we wanted. The guards would let us sneak it in, you know? But this one time I took some of it and, *híjola,* I got *stoned, ese.* I was reading a copy of *La Voz* my *jefita* sent me. And there was this picture of you in there. So I said, 'If I ever get out, I'm gonna go see old Zeta.' So that's why I told the dudes from PINTO I'd take care of you."

Now Sailor Boy and Pelon sit together in the first row, waiting for me. Next to them are the other ex-cons who belong to the recently-formed organization. The Pintos wear their knife and chain scars from the old gang wars of their youth. During those days in the housing projects, the urban reservations set aside for Chicanos, these *vatos* would murder one of their own at least weekly. These children of the slums, offspring of reds and wine and welfare, had gone to jail and come out to find the new revolution just waiting for them, the original rebels. Now they could take it out on the pigs and be called hero instead of *loco.* Now they were former political prisoners, not ex-cons. Now they could take up a man like Buffalo Z. Brown and all his bullshit, and shove it in the face of those same white men who'd been giving them a hard time from the day they were born.

I am assuring the defendants that all goes well. "Hey, *ese,*" Gilbert says, "What's the matter? You look like shit. Are you sick or something?" The others are looking at me curiously.

"Forget it," I say. "I just need some spring air. See you in an hour."

I grab my briefcase, which is empty except for a gun, and push off. Sailor Boy joins me by the elevator. I can't go anywhere alone. As we go down from the seventh floor of the Hall of Justice, he talks about the film. During the Moratorium, he was in the slam. All that he know came from the papers and stories from the *vatos* who were there. This is the first time he has *seen, felt* the action for what it was. He is excited.

"Did you see that?" he says. "They really *did* it, you know? I wish I was there. . . . "

"Yeah."

"Hey, I forgot. You weren't there, either. Look, why don't we drive over to the park right now? We can look around and . . . you'll feel better there, I know it."

"No."

"OK, *ese,* whatever you say."

We walk out of the courthouse into the dirt and slime. Even in spring, the smog sits on the city like moldy orange juice. I look back. For years I have been walking in and out of that building, into the icebox of justice and then out into the garbage. Nobody has to tell me I'm sick. Nobody has to say, Zeta, you look like shit. I stand there, staring backward like an idiot. Sailor Boy is gaping at me. People, lawyers on their way to lunch pass us. And he wants to go to Laguna Park. The place where I once stood on a bench hollering about land and war and blood. The place where I was brought later in late August of last year, when I returned from Acapulco. . . .

August 30, 1970. Gilbert and Pelon had picked me up at the airport. On the plane I had to think it all out, what I will say to them. For years the three of us have gotten drunk together, laughed and fought together. Nobody else in the *movida* knows me like they do. Yet I am in trouble for leaving, for dropping out.

Zanzibar is dead. Corky and Gilbert and others are up for the rap. So I am back.

Shit, it is obvious to me that if I never went to Acapulco, everything would still be the same. Someone would be dead. Someone else among us would be framed for it and I would defend him. On that plane I got one of the biggest headaches in my life. I'm doing what must be done. Why should anybody give me trouble about what I do with the rest of my life? Is this what we've all been fighting for?

After the big hugs, I follow them out of the airline lobby to my car. Gilbert's leg drags slightly as he walks, from a fleshwound, an FBI bullet. Pelon has been driving the Mustang while I was away. From the first moment I see their eyes, I know they are with me. But Gilbert, the fat frog, is troubled; Pelon is glum. They want me to talk to them. Soon we are piled again into my blue beauty, heading east on the freeway. They tell me the events of the last few months, the day Zanzibar was killed in particular.

"Jesus Christ," I say. "Sounds like somebody masterminded the perfect crime."

"What's that, *ese*?" Gilbert says. He sits in the back. I am next to Pelon who is driving us through the afternoon. After the jungle and houses of Mexico, everything I see in LA looks dull and colorless.

"If anybody set out to destroy the Chicano movement, he couldn't do better than murdering Zanzibar and hanging it on Corky. Corky makes things happen and Zanzibar makes what's happened important."

"Corky wasn't busted for murder," Pelon says.

"So what? Roland's dead and Corky's out of action. . . . Gilbert here has to watch his step. Plus the others."

"Eh, *ese*, do you, uh, want to go home before you meet with the other defendants?" Gilbert asks. "The *vatos* are wondering about whether, uh, if they want you to. . . . " He breaks off. I have never heard him talk like that before, halting and tripping himself. Suddenly, a flash of inspiration!

"Look, you guys." I am getting mad, I still have my headache. "What the fuck do I have to apologize for? You're always telling me how you're going to shoot your arms off with junk after the revolution. Nobody is going to tell you what to do. I've been a lawyer for three years now. THREE YEARS! You know I don't want to be no fucking lawyer! So when everything's cool, I go to see my brother and relax. Nobody has the right to beef! Here I am and nothing's any different!"

"Shit, *ese*," Gilbert says, "I know that. But some of the others. . . . "

"Sure, Zeta, that's what we've been saying," Pelon says.

"All right! Where is everybody?"

"Waiting for us at the park," Gilbert says. "Except Corky. He's still in."

"Let's go."

We drive to Laguna Park, passing by the ruins of Whittier Boulevard. Not as bad as Watts, but still bad. A little reminder from the people that a war is in progress. Pelon and Gilbert carry on a running commentary. When we pass the Silver Dollar Bar where Zanzibar was killed, I see it's boarded up.

We meet Ramirez, Raza, Waterbuffalo and Bullwinkle at one of the benches. We all have known and respected each other. Aside from Corky, only Elena Lowrider isn't here. The rest of the park is pretty much deserted.

"Hey, man," Bullwinkle leads off. "What the fuck's with you?"

"Acapulco!" snorts Waterbuffalo. "*Vatos* are dying and you're off gettin' a tan."

This is it. With more energy than I have ever used at one time, I shout: SHUT UP!

There is a surprising silence. I calm down, just a little.

"Listen, you guys. I'm no kamikaze! Are you? Do you *want* to die? I'm a writer, yeah, and a singer of songs. I just happen to be a lawyer and a fighter. If I'm not all that, I'm dead! What the hell are we fighting for? For land and to live just like we want. Fuck it! You think I *knew* what was coming down? You think I *planned* to disappear just then? After two and a half years, just because I split for a while, just because I go around and screw who I want to, you think I'm not in this fight whole hog? You're all a bunch of goddamn idiots if you think that! No wonder you were caught. . . . "

For half an hour I rail and rant. I tell them exactly where I'm at. And when I'm finished, they ask me to defend them.

They also ask me about Corky: how does he stand? Can they trust him? Aside from Cesar Chavez, he has the biggest reputation as the toughest Chicano in America. But he is an outsider, from Denver. Can they all work together? I tell them not to worry, that Corky is a man to be trusted.

But they still want to meet him and talk with him personally. Since only Corky is not out on bail, they haven't been able to see him. After I talk with them, they *still* want to see him. They want to check out if *they* can trust him. Which means they don't trust me anymore. They just *need* me. I promise to arrange a meeting in a few days and get to work on the cases. Then we split.

The three of us drive to my house on Sixth Street. The silence in the car is heavy. The prospect of another long trial makes me sick. The togetherness of the first few years seems gone. Now that Zanzibar is dead, there is nobody to tell our story to the world. I am spinning around in emptiness, thinking of what my brother Jesus told me. Who have we killed? Just how heavy *are* we? I am confused, but by the time we reach the house I have made two decisions. When I have finished this trial, I will write my book. Without fail. And win or lose, I will destroy the courthouse where the *gabachos* have made me dance these last years with lead in my belly and tears in my heart.

1973

SAM SHEPARD

Motel Chronicles

He tried to boost an absolutely worthless print of a Cottonwood Tree stranded in a dry desert basin from the
Chateau Marmont Hotel on Sunset Boulevard.

They caught him with it in the parking lot, cramming it
into the bed of his pickup.

When they asked him why, he told them he wasn't sure why.
He told them it gave him this feeling.

He told them he saw himself inside this picture lying on his
back underneath the Cottonwood.

He said he recognized the tree from an old dream and
that the dream was based on a real tree he dimly remembered from a long time ago in his childhood.

He remembered lying down underneath this tree and
staring up through the silver leaves.

He remembered voices from those leaves but he couldn't
remember what the voices said or who they belonged to.

He told them he was hoping the picture would bring the
whole thing back.

I 've about seen
all the nose jobs
capped teeth
and silly-cone tits
I can handle.

I'm heading back
to my natural woman

1982

JOHN FANTE

Ask the Dust

O N E   N I G H T I was sitting on the bed in my hotel room on Bunker Hill, down in the very middle of Los Angeles. It was an important night in my life, because I had to make a decision about the hotel. Either I paid up or I got out: that was what the note said, the note the landlady had put under my door. A great problem, deserving acute attention. I solved it by turning out the lights and going to bed.

In the morning I awoke, decided that I should do more physical exercise, and began at once. I did several bending exercises. Then I washed my teeth, tasted blood, saw pink on the toothbrush, remembered the advertisements, and decided to go out and get some coffee.

I went to the restaurant where I always went to the restaurant and I sat down on the stool before the long counter and ordered coffee. It tasted pretty much like coffee, but it wasn't worth the nickel. Sitting there I smoked a couple of cigarets, read the box scores of the American League games, scrupulously avoided the box scores of National League games, and noted with satisfaction that Joe DiMaggio was still a credit to the Italian people, because he was leading the league in batting.

A great hitter, that DiMaggio. I walked out of the restaurant, stood before an imaginary pitcher, and swatted a home run over the fence. Then I walked down the street toward Angel's Flight, wondering what I would do that day. But there was nothing to do, and so I decided to walk around the town.

I walked down Olive Street past a dirty yellow apartment house that was still wet like a blotter from last night's fog, and I thought of my friends Ethie and Carl, who were from Detroit and had lived there, and I remembered the night Carl hit Ethie because she was going to have a baby, and he didn't want a baby. But they had the baby and that's all there was to that. And I remembered the inside of that apartment, how it smelled of mice and dust, and the old women who sat in the lobby on hot afternoons, and the old woman with the pretty legs. Then there was the elevator man, a broken man from Milwaukee, who seemed to sneer every time you called your floor, as though you were such a fool for choosing that particular floor, the elevator man who always had a tray of sandwiches in the elevator, and a pulp magazine.

Then I went down the hill on Olive Street, past the horrible frame houses reeking with murder stories, and on down Olive to the Philharmonic Auditorium, and I remembered how I'd gone there with Helen to listen to the Don Cossack Choral Group, and how I got bored and we had a fight because of it, and I remembered what Helen wore that day—a white dress, and how it made me sing at the loins when I touched it. Oh that Helen—but not here.

And so I was down on Fifth and Olive, where the big street cars chewed your ears with their noise, and the smell of gasoline made the sight of the palm trees seem sad, and the black pavement still wet from the fog of the night before.

So now I was in front of the Biltmore Hotel, walking along the line of yellow cabs, with all the cab drivers asleep except the driver near the main door, and I wondered about these fellows and their fund of information, and I remembered the time Ross and I got an address from one of them, how he leered salaciously and then took us to Temple Street, of all places, and whom did we see but two very unattractive ones, and Ross went all the way, but I sat in the parlor and played the phonograph and was scared and lonely.

I was passing the doorman of the Biltmore, and I hated him at once, with his yellow braids and six feet of height and all that dignity, and now a black automobile drove to the curb, and a man got out. He looked rich; and then a woman got out, and she was beautiful, her fur was silver fox, and she was a song across the sidewalk and inside the swinging doors, and I thought oh boy for a little of that, just a day and a night of that, and she was a dream as I walked along, her perfume still in the wet morning air.

Then a great deal of time passed as I stood in front of a pipe shop and looked, and the whole world faded except that window and I stood and smoked them all, and saw myself a great author with that natty Italian briar, and a cane, stepping out of a big black car, and she was there too, proud as hell of me, the lady in the silver fox fur. We registered and then we had cocktails and then we danced awhile, and then we had another cocktail and I recited some lines from Sanskrit, and the world was so wonderful, because every two minutes some gorgeous one gazed at me, the great author, and nothing would do but I had to autograph her menu, and the silver fox girl was very jealous.

Los Angeles, give me some of you! Los Angeles come to me the way I came to you, my feet over your streets, you pretty town I loved you so much, you sad flower in the sand, you pretty town.

A day and another day and the day before, and the library with the big boys in the shelves, old Dreiser, old Mencken, all the boys down there, and I went to see them, Hya Dreiser, Hya Mencken, Hya, hya: there's a place for me, too, and it begins with B, in the B shelf, Arturo Bandini, make way for Arturo Bandini, his slot for his book, and I sat at the table and just looked at the place where my book would be, right there close to Arnold Bennett; not much that Arnold Bennett, but I'd be there to sort of bolster up the B's, old Arturo Bandini, one of the boys, until some girl came along, some scent of perfume through the fiction room, some click of high heels to break up the monotony of my fame. Gala day, gala dream!

But the landlady, the white-haired landlady kept writing those notes: she was from Bridgeport, Connecticut, her husband had died and she was all alone in the world and she didn't trust anybody, she couldn't afford to, she told me so, and she told me I'd have to pay. It was mounting like the national debt, I'd have to pay or leave, every cent of it—five weeks overdue, twenty dollars, and if I didn't she'd hold my trunks; only I didn't have any trunks, I only had a suitcase and it was cardboard without even a strap, because the strap was around my belly holding up my pants, and that wasn't much of a job, because there wasn't much left of my pants.

"I just got a letter from my agent," I told her. "My agent in New York. He says I sold another one; he doesn't say where, but he says he's got one sold. So don't worry Mrs. Hargraves, don't you fret, I'll have it in a day or so."

But she couldn't believe a liar like me. It wasn't really a lie; it was a wish, not a lie, and maybe it wasn't even a wish, maybe it was a fact, and the only way to find out was watch the mailman, watch him closely, check his mail as he laid it on the desk in the lobby, ask him point blank if he had anything for Bandini. But I didn't have to ask after six months at that hotel. He saw me coming and he always nodded yes or no before I asked: no, three million times; yes, once.

One day a beautiful letter came. Oh, I got a lot of letters, but this was the only beautiful letter, and it came in the morning, and it said (he was talking about *The Little Dog Laughed*) he had read *The Little Dog Laughed* and liked it; he said, Mr. Bandini, if ever I saw a genius, you are it. His name was Leonardo, a great Italian critic, only he was not known as a critic, he was just a man in West Virginia, but he was great and he was a critic, and he died. He was dead when my airmail letter got to West Virginia, and his sister sent my letter back. She wrote a beautiful letter too, she was a pretty good critic too, telling me Leonardo had died of consumption but he was happy to the end, and one of the last things he did was sit up in bed and write me about *The Little Dog Laughed:* a dream out of life, but very important; Leonardo, dead now, a saint in heaven, equal to any apostle of the twelve.

Everybody in the hotel read *The Little Dog Laughed,* everybody: a story to make you die holding the page, and it wasn't about a dog, either: a clever story, screaming poetry. And the great editor, none but J. C. Hackmuth with his name signed like Chinese said in a letter: a great story and I'm proud to print it. Mrs. Hargraves read it and I was a different man in her eyes thereafter. I got to stay on in that hotel, not shoved out in the cold, only often it was in the heat, on account of *The Little Dog Laughed.* Mrs. Grainger in 345, a Christian Scientist (wonderful hips, but kinda old) from Battle Creek, Michigan, sitting in the lobby waiting to die, and *The Little Dog Laughed* brought her back to the earth, and that look in her eyes made me know it was right and I was right, but I was hoping she would ask about my finances, how I was getting along, and then I thought why not ask her to lend you a five spot, but I didn't and I walked away snapping my fingers in disgust.

The hotel was called the Alta Loma. It was built on a hillside in reverse, there on the crest of Bunker Hill, built against the decline of the hill, so that the main floor was on the level with the street but the tenth floor was downstairs ten levels. If you had room 862, you got in the elevator and went down eight floors, and if you wanted to go down in the truck room, you didn't go down but up to the attic, one floor above the main floor.

Oh for a Mexican girl! I used to think of her all the time, my Mexican girl. I didn't have one, but the streets were full of them, the Plaza and Chinatown were afire wtih them, and in my fashion they were mine, this one and that one, and some day when another check came it would be a fact. Meanwhile it was free and they were Aztec princesses and Mayan princesses, the peon girls in the Grand Central Market, in the Church of Our Lady, and I even went to Mass to look at them. That was sacrilegious conduct but it was better than not going to Mass at all, so that when I wrote home to Colorado to my mother I could write with truth. Dear Mother: I went to Mass last Sunday. Down in the Grand Central Market I bumped into the princesses accidentally on purpose. It gave me a chance to speak to them, and I smiled and said excuse me. Those beautiful girls, so happy when you acted like a gentleman and all of that, just to touch them and carry the memory of it back to my room, where dust gathered upon my typewriter and Pedro the mouse sat in his hole, his black eyes watching me through that time of dream and reverie.

Pedro the mouse, a good mouse but never domesticated, refusing to be petted or house-broken. I saw him the first time I walked into my room, and that was during my hey-day, when *The Little Dog Laughed* was in the current August issue. It was five months ago, the day I got to town by bus from Colorado with a hundred and fifty dollars in my pocket and big plans in my head. I had a philosophy in those days. I was a lover of man and beast alike, and Pedro was no exception; but cheese got expensive, Pedro called all his friends, the room swarmed with them, and I had to quit it and feed them bread. They didn't like bread. I had spoiled them and they went elsewhere, all but Pedro the ascetic who was content to eat the pages of an old Gideon Bible.

Ah, that first day! Mrs. Hargraves opened the door to my room, and there it was, with a red carpet on the floor, pictures of the English countryside on the walls, and a shower adjoining. The room was down on the sixth floor, room 678, up near the front of the hill, so that my window was on a level with the green hillside and there was no need for a key, for the window was always open. Through that window I saw my first palm tree, not six feet away, and sure enough I thought of Palm Sunday and Egypt and Cleopatra, but the palm was blackish at its branches, stained by carbon monoxide coming out of the Third Street Tunnel, its crusted trunk choked with dust and sand that blew in from the Mojave and Santa Ana deserts.

Dear Mother, I used to write home to Colorado, Dear Mother, things are definitely looking up. A big editor was in town and I had lunch with him and we have signed a contract for a number of short stories, but I won't try to bore you with all the details, dear mother, because I know you're not interested in writing, and I know Papa isn't, but it levels down to a swell contract, only it doesn't begin for a couple of months. So send me ten dollars, mother, send me five, mother dear, because the editor (I'd tell you his name only I know you're not interested in such things) is all set to start me out on the biggest project he's got.

Dear Mother, and Dear Hackmuth, the great editor—they got most of my mail, practically all of my mail. Old Hackmuth with his scowl and his hair parted in the middle, great Hackmuth with a pen like a sword, his picture was on my wall autographed with his signature that looked Chinese. Hya Hackmuth, I used to say, Jesus how you can write! Then the lean days came, and Hackmuth got big letters from me. My God, Mr. Hackmuth, something's wrong with me: the old zip is gone and I can't write anymore. Do you think, Mr. Hackmuth, that the climate here has anything to do with it? Please advise. Do you think, Mr. Hackmuth, that I write as well as William Faulkner? Please advise. Do you think, Mr. Hackmuth, that sex has anything to do with it, because, Mr. Hackmuth, because, because, and I told Hackmuth everything. I told him about the blonde girl I met in the park. I told him how I worked it, how the blonde girl tumbled. I told him the whole story, only it wasn't true, it was a crazy lie—but it was something. It was writing, keeping in touch with the great, and he always answered. Oh boy, he was swell! He answered right off, a great man responding to the problems of a man of talent. Nobody got that many letters from Hackmuth, nobody but me, and I used to take them out and read them over, and kiss them. I'd stand before Hackmuth's picture crying out of both eyes, telling him he picked a good one this time, a great one, a Bandini, Arturo Bandini, me.

The lean days of determination. That was the word for it, determination: Arturo Bandini in front of his typewriter two full days in succession, determined to succeed; but it didn't work, the longest siege of hard and fast determination in his life, and not one line done, only two words written over and over across the page, up and down, the same words: palm tree, palm tree, palm tree, a battle to the death between the palm tree and me, and the palm tree won: see it out there swaying in the blue air, creaking sweetly in the blue air. The palm tree won after two fighting days, and I crawled out of the window and sat at the foot of the tree. Time passed, a moment or two, and I slept, little brown ants carousing in the hair on my legs.

1939

HELEN HUNT JACKSON

Ramona

THE SEÑORA Moreno's house was one of the best specimens to be found in California of the representative house of the half barbaric, half elegant, wholly generous and free-handed life led there by Mexican men and women of degree in the early part of this century, under the rule of the Spanish and Mexican viceroys, when the laws of the Indies were still the law of the land, and its old name, "New Spain," was an ever-present link and stimulus to the warmest memories and deepest patriotisms of its people.

It was a picturesque life, with more of sentiment and gayety in it, more also that was truly dramatic, more romance, than will ever be seen again on those sunny shores. The aroma of it all lingers there still; industries and inventions have not yet slain it; it will last out its century,—in fact, it can never be quite lost, so long as there is left standing one such house as the Señora Moreno's.

When the house was built, General Moreno owned all the land within a radius of forty miles,—forty miles westward, down the valley to the sea; forty miles eastward, into the San Fernando Mountains; and good forty miles more or less along the coast. The boundaries were not very strictly defined; there was no occasion, in those happy days, to reckon land by inches. It might be asked, perhaps, just how General Moreno owned all this land, and the question might not be easy to answer. It was not and could not be answered to the satisfaction of the United States Land Commission, which, after the surrender of California, undertook to sift and adjust Mexican land titles; and that was the way it had come about that the Señora Moreno now called herself a poor woman. Tract after tract, her lands had been taken away from her; it looked for a time as if nothing would be left. Every one of the claims based on deeds of gift from Governor Pio Pico, her husband's most intimate friend, was disallowed. They all went by the board in one batch, and took away from the Señora in a day the greater part of her best pasture-lands. They were lands which had belonged to the Bonaventura Mission, and lay along the coast at the mouth of the valley down which the little stream which ran past her house went to the sea; and it had been a great pride and delight to the Señora, when she was young, to ride that forty miles by her husband's side, all the way on their own lands, straight from their house to their own strip of shore. No wonder she believed the Americans thieves, and spoke of them always as hounds. The people of the United States have never in the least realized that the taking possession of California was not only a conquering of Mexico, but a conquering of California as well; that the real bitterness of the surrender was not so much to the empire which gave up the country, as to the country itself which was given up. Provinces passed back and forth in that way, helpless in the hands of great powers, have all the ignominy and humiliation of defeat, with none of the dignities or compensations of the transaction.

Mexico saved much by her treaty, spite of having to acknowledge herself beaten; but California lost all. Words cannot tell the sting of such a transfer. It is a marvel that a Mexican remained in the country; probably none did, except those who were absolutely forced to it.

Luckily for the Señora Moreno, her title to the lands midway in the valley was better than to those lying to the east and the west, which had once belonged to the missions of San Fernando and Bonaventura; and after all the claims, counter-claims, petitions, appeals, and adjudications were ended, she still was left in undisputed possession of what would have been thought by any new-comer into the country to be a handsome estate, but which seemed to the despoiled and indignant Señora a pitiful fragment of one. Moreover, she declared that she should never feel secure of a foot of even this. Any day, she said, the United States Government might send out a new Land Commission to examine the decrees of the first, and revoke such as they saw fit. Once a thief, always a thief. Nobody need feel himself safe under American rule. There was no knowing what might happen any day; and year by year the lines of sadness, resentment, anxiety, and antagonism deepened on the Señora's fast aging face.

It gave her unspeakable satisfaction, when the Commissioners, laying out a road down the valley, ran it at the back of her house instead of past the front. "It is well," she said. "Let their travel be where it belongs, behind our kitchens; and no one have sight of the front doors of our houses, except friends who have come to visit us." Her enjoyment of this never flagged. Whenever she saw, passing the place, wagons or carriages belonging to the hated Americans, it gave her a distinct thrill of pleasure to think that the house turned its back on them. She would like always to be able to do the same herself; but whatever she, by policy or in business, might be forced to do, the old house, at any rate, would always keep the attitude of contempt,—its face turned away.

One other pleasure she provided herself with, soon after this road was opened,—a pleasure in which religious devotion and race antagonism were so closely blended that it would have puzzled the subtlest of priests to decide whether her act were a sin or a virtue. She caused to be set up, upon every one of the soft rounded hills which made the beautiful rolling sides of that part of the valley, a large wooden cross; not a hill in sight of her house left without the sacred emblem of her faith. "That the heretics may know, when they go by, that they are on the estate of a good Catholic," she said, "and that the faithful may be reminded to pray. There have been miracles of conversion wrought on the most hardened by a sudden sight of the Blessed Cross."

There they stood, summer and winter, rain and shine, the silent, solemn, outstretched arms, and became landmarks to many a guide-less traveller who had been told that his way would be by the first turn to the left or the right, after passing the last one of the Señora Moreno's crosses, which he couldn't miss seeing. And who shall say that it did not often happen that the crosses bore a sudden message to some idle heart journeying by, and thus justified the pious half of the Señora's impulse? Certain it is, that many a good Catholic halted and crossed himself when he first beheld them, in the lonely places, standing out in sudden relief against the blue sky; and if he said a swift short prayer at the sight, was he not so much the better?

The house was of adobe, low, with a wide veranda on the three sides of the inner court, and a still broader one across the entire front, which looked to the south. These verandas, especially those on the inner court, were supplementary rooms to the house. The greater part of the family life went on in them. Nobody stayed inside the walls, except when it was necessary. All the kitchen work, except the actual cooking, was done here, in front of the kitchen doors and windows. Babies slept, were washed, sat in the dirt, and played, on the veranda. The women said their prayers, took their naps, and wove their lace there. Old Juanita shelled her beans there, and threw the pods down on the tile floor, till towards night they were sometimes piled up high around her, like corn-husks at a husking. The herdsmen and shepherds smoked there, lounged there, trained their dogs there; there the young made love, and the old dozed; the benches, which ran the entire length of the walls, were worn into hollows, and shone like satin; the tiles floors also were broken and sunk in places, making little wells, which filled up in times of hard rains, and were then an invaluable addition to the children's resources for amusement, and also to the comfort of the dogs, cats, and fowls, who picked about among them, taking sips from each.

The arched veranda along the front was a delightsome place. It must have been eighty feet long, at least, for the doors of five large rooms opened on it. The two westernmost rooms had been added on, and made four steps higher than the others; which gave to that end of the veranda the look of a balcony, or loggia. Here the Señora kept her flowers; great red water-jars, hand-made by the Indians of San Luis Obispo Mission, stood in close rows against the walls, and in them were always growing fine geraniums, carnations, and yellow-flowered musk. The Señora's passion for musk she had inherited from her mother. It was so strong that she sometimes wondered at it; and one day, as she sat with Father Salvierderra in the veranda, she picked a handful of the blossoms, and giving them to him, said, "I do not know why it is, but it seems to me if I were dead I could be brought to life by the smell of musk."

"It is in your blood, Señora," the old monk replied. "When I was last in your father's house in Seville, your mother sent for me to her room, and under her window was a stone balcony full of growing musk, which so filled the room with its odor that I was like to faint. But she said it cured her of diseases, and without it she fell ill. You were a baby then."

"Yes," cried the Señora, "but I recollect that balcony. I recollect being lifted up to a window, and looking down into a bed of blooming yellow flowers; but I did not know what they were. How strange!"

"No. Not strange, daughter," replied Father Salvierderra. "It would have been stranger if you had not acquired the taste, thus drawing it in with the mother's milk. It would behoove mothers to remember this far more than they do."

Besides the geraniums and carnations and musk in the red jars, there were many sorts of climbing vines,—some coming from the ground, and twining around the pillars of the veranda; some growing in great bowls, swung by cords from the roof of the veranda, or set on shelves against the walls. These bowls were of gray stone, hollowed and polished, shining smooth inside and out. They also had been made by the Indians, nobody knew how many ages ago, scooped and polished by the patient creatures, with only stones for tools.

Among these vines, singing from morning till night, hung the Señora's canaries and finches, half a dozen of each, all of different generations, raised by the Señora. She was never without a young bird-family on hand; and all the way from Bonaventura to Monterey, it was thought a piece of good luck to come into possession of a canary or finch of Señora Moreno's raising.

Between the veranda and the river meadows, out on which it looked, all was garden, orange grove, and almond orchard; the orange grove always green, never without snowy bloom or golden fruit; the garden never without flowers, summer or winter; and the almond orchard, in early spring, a fluttering canopy of pink and white petals, which, seen from the hills on the opposite side of the river, looked as if rosy sunrise clouds had fallen, and become tangled in the tree-tops. On either hand stretched away other orchards,—peach, apricot, pear, apple pomegranate; and beyond these, vineyards. Nothing was to be seen but verdure or bloom or fruit, at whatever time of year you sat on the Señora's south veranda.

A wide straight walk shaded by a trellis so knotted and twisted with grapevines that little was to be seen of the trellis wood-work, led straight down from the veranda steps, through the middle of the garden, to a little brook at the foot of it. Across this brook, in the shade of a dozen gnarled old willow-trees, were set the broad flat stone washboards on which was done all the family washing. No long dawdling, and no running away from work on the part of the maids, thus close to the eye of the Señora at the upper end of the garden; and it they had known how picturesque they looked there, kneeling on the grass, lifting the dripping linen out of the water, rubbing it back and forth on the stones, sousing it, wringing it, splashing the clear water in each other's faces, they would have been content to stay at the washing day in and day out, for there was always somebody to look on from above. Hardly a day passed that the Señora had not visitors. She was still a person of note; her house the natural resting-place for all who journeyed through the valley; and whoever came, spent all of his time, when not eating, sleeping, or walking over the place, sitting with the Señora on the sunny veranda. Few days in winter were cold enough, and in summer the day must be hot indeed to drive the Señora and her friends indoors. There stood on the veranda three carved oaken chairs, and a carved bench, also of oak, which had been brought to the Señora for safe keeping by the faithful old sacristan of San Luis Rey, at the time of the occupation of that Mission by the United States troops, soon after the conquest of California. Aghast at the sacrilegious acts of the soldiers, who were quartered in the very church itself, and amused themselves by making targets of the eyes and noses of the saints' statues, the sacristan, stealthily, day by day and night after night, bore out of the church all that he dared to remove, burying some articles in cottonwood copses, hiding others in his own poor little hovel, until he had wagon-loads of sacred treasures. Then, still more stealthily, he carried them, a few at a time, concealed in the bottom of a cart, under a load of hay or of brush, to the house of the Señora, who felt herself deeply honored by his confidence, and received everything as a sacred trust, to be given back into the hands of the Church again, whenever the Missions should be restored, of which at that time all Catholics had good hope. And so it had come about that no bedroom in the Señora's house was without a picture or a statue of a saint or of the Madonna; and some had two; and in the little chapel in the garden the altar was surrounded by a really imposing row of holy and apostolic figures, which had looked down on the splendid ceremonies of the San Luis Rey Mission, in Father Peyri's time, no more benignly than they now did on the humbler worship of the Señora's family in its diminished estate. That one had lost an eye, another an arm, that the once brilliant colors of the drapery were now faded and shabby, only enhanced the tender reverence with which the Señora knelt before them, her eyes filling with indignant tears at thought of the heretic hands which had wrought such defilement. Even the crumbling wreaths which had been placed on some of the statues' heads at the time of the last ceremonial at which they had figured in the Mission, had been brought away with them by the devout sacristan, and the Señora had replaced each one, holding it only a degree less sacred that the statue itself.

This chapel was dearer to the Señora than her house. It had been built by the General in the second year of their married life. In it her four children had been christened, and from it all but one, her handsome Felipe, had been buried while they were yet infants. In the General's time, while the estate was at its best, and hundreds of Indians living within its borders, there was many a Sunday when the scene to be witnessed there was like the scenes at the Missions,—the chapel full of kneeling men and women; those who could not find room inside kneeling on the garden walks outside; Father Salvierderra, in gorgeous vestments, coming, at close of the services, slowly down the aisle, the close-packed rows of worshippers parting to right and left to let him through, all looking up eagerly for his blessing, women giving him offerings of fruit or flowers, and holding up their babies that he might lay his hands on their heads. No one but Father Salvierderra had ever officiated in the Moreno chapel, or heard the confession of a Moreno. He was a Franciscan, one of the few now left in the country; so revered and beloved by all who had come under his influence, that they would wait long months without the offices of the Church, rather than confess their sins or confide their perplexities to any one else. From this deep-seated attachment on the part of the Indians and the older Mexican families in the country to the Franciscan Order, there had grown up, not unnaturally, some jealousy of them in the minds of the later-come secular priests, and the position of the few monks left was not wholly a pleasant one. It had even been rumored that they were to be forbidden to continue longer their practice of going up and down the country, ministering everywhere; were to be compelled to restrict their labors to their own colleges at Santa Barbara and Santa Inez. When something to this effect was one day said in the Señora Moreno's presence, two scarlet spots sprang on her cheeks, and before she bethought herself, she exclaimed, "That day, I burn down my chapel!"

Luckily, nobody but Felipe heard the rash threat, and his exclamation of unbounded astonishment recalled the Señora to herself.

"I spoke rashly, my son," she said. "The Church is to be obeyed always; but the Franciscan Fathers are responsible to no one but the Superior of their own order; and there is no one in this land who has the authority to forbid their journeying and ministering to whoever desires their offices. As for these Catalan priests who are coming in here, I cannot abide them. No Catalan but has bad blood in his veins!"

There was every reason in the world why the Señora should be thus warmly attached to the Franciscan Order. From her earliest recollections the gray gown and cowl had been familiar to her eyes, and had represented the things which she was taught to hold most sacred and dear. Father Salvierderra himself had come from Mexico to Monterey in the same ship which had brought her father to be the commandante of the Santa Barbara Presidio; and her best-beloved uncle, her father's eldest brother, was at that time the Superior of the Santa Barbara Mission. The sentiment and romance of her youth were almost equally divided between the gayeties, excitements, adornments of the life at the Presidio, and the ceremonies and devotions of the life at the Mission. She was famed as the most beautiful girl in the country. Men of the army, men of the navy, and men of the Church, alike adored her. Her name was a toast from Monterey to San Diego. When at last she was wooed and won by Felipe Moreno, one of the most distinguished of the Mexican Generals, her wedding ceremonies were the most splendid ever seen in the country. The right tower of the Mission church at Santa Barbara had been just completed, and it was arranged that the consecration of this tower should take place at the time of her wedding, and that her wedding feast should be spread in the long outside corridor of the Mission building. The whole country, far and near, was bid. The feast lasted three days; open tables to everybody; singing, dancing, eating, drinking, and making merry. At that time there were long streets of Indian houses stretching eastward from the Mission; before each of these houses was built a booth of green boughs. The Indians, as well as the Fathers from all the other Missions, were invited to come. The Indians came in bands, singing songs and bringing gifts. As they appeared, the Santa Barbara Indians went out to meet them, also singing, bearing gifts, and strewing seeds on the ground, in token of welcome. The young Señora and her bridegroom, splendidly clothed, were seen of all, and greeted, whenever they appeared, by showers of seeds and grains and blossoms. On the third day, still in their wedding attire, and bearing lighted candles in their hands, they walked with the monks in a procession, round and round the new tower, the monks chanting, and sprinkling incense and holy water on its walls, the ceremony seeming to all devout beholders to give a blessed consecration to the union of the young pair as well as to the newly completed tower. After this they journeyed in state, accompanied by several of the General's aids and officers, and by two Franciscan Fathers, up to Monterey, stopping on their way at all the Missions, and being warmly welcomed and entertained at each.

General Moreno was much beloved by both army and Church. In many of the frequent clashings between the military and the ecclesiastical powers he, being as devout and enthusiastic a Catholic as he was zealous and enthusiastic a soldier, had had the good fortune to be of material assistance to each party. The Indians also knew his name well, having heard it many times mentioned with public thanksgivings in the Mission churches, after some signal service he had rendered to the Fathers either in Mexico or Monterey. And now, by taking as his bride the daughter of a distinguished officer, and the niece of the Santa Barbara Superior, he had linked himself anew to the two dominant powers and interests of the country.

When they reached San Luis Obispo, the whole Indian population turned out to meet them, the Padre walking at the head. As they approached the Mission doors the Indians swarmed closer and closer and still closer, took the General's horse by the head, and finally almost by actual force compelled him to allow himself to be lifted into a blanket, held high up by twenty strong men; and thus he was borne up the steps, across the corridor, and into the Padre's room. It was a position ludicrously undignified in itself, but the General submitted to it good-naturedly.

"Oh, let them do it, if they like," he cried, laughingly, to Padre Martinez, who was endeavoring to quiet the Indians and hold them back. "Let them do it. It pleases the poor creatures."

On the morning of their departure, the good Padre, having exhausted all his resources for entertaining his distinguished guests, caused to be driven past the corridors, for their inspection, all the poultry belonging to the Mission. The procession took an hour to pass. For music, there was the squeaking, cackling, hissing, gobbling, crowing, quacking of the fowls, combined with the screaming, scolding, and whip-cracking of the excited Indian marshals of the lines. First came the turkeys, then the roosters, then the white hens, then the black, and then the yellow, next the ducks, and at the tail of the spectacle long files of geese, some strutting, some half flying and hissing in resentment and terror at the unwonted coercions to which they were subjected. The Indians had been hard at work all night capturing, sorting, assorting, and guarding the rank and file of their novel pageant. It would be safe to say that a droller sight never was seen, and never will be, on the Pacific coast or any other. Before it was done with, the General and his bride had nearly died with laughter; and the General could never allude to it without laughing almost as heartily again.

At Monterey they were more magnificently fêted; at the Presidio, at the Mission, on board Spanish, Mexican, and Russian ships lying in harbor, balls, dances, bull-fights, dinners, all that the country knew of festivity, was lavished on the beautiful and winning young bride. The belles of the coast, from San Diego up, had all gathered at Monterey for these gayeties, but not one of them could be for a moment compared to her. This was the beginning of the Señora's life as a married woman. She was then just twenty. A close observer would have seen even then, underneath the joyous smile, the laughing eye, the merry voice, a look thoughtful, tender, earnest, at times enthusiastic. This look was the reflection of those qualities in her, then hardly aroused, which made her, as years developed her character and stormy fates thickened around her life, the unflinching comrade of her soldier husband, the passionate adherent of the Church. Through wars, insurrections, revolutions, downfalls, Spanish, Mexican, civil, ecclesiastical, her standpoint, her poise, remained the same. She simply grew more and more proudly, passionately, a Spaniard and a Moreno; more and more staunchly and fierily a Catholic, and a lover of the Franciscans.

During the height of the despoiling and plundering of the Missions, under the Secularization Act, she was for a few years almost beside herself. More than once she journeyed alone, when the journey was by no means without danger, to Monterey, to stir up the Prefect of the Missions to more energetic action, to implore the governmental authorities to interfere, and protect the Church's property. It was largely in consequence of her eloquent entreaties that Governor Micheltorena issued his bootless order, restoring to the Church all the Missions south of San Luis Obispo. But this order cost Micheltorena his political head, and General Moreno was severely wounded in one of the skirmishes of the insurrection which drove Micheltorena out of the country.

In silence and bitter humiliation the Señora nursed her husband back to health again, and resolved to meddle no more in the affairs of her unhappy country and still more unhappy church. As year by year she saw the ruin of the Missions steadily going on, their vast properties melting away, like dew before the sun, in the hands of dishonest administrators and politicians, the Church powerless to contend with the unprincipled greed in high places, her beloved Franciscan Fathers driven from the country or dying of starvation at their posts, she submitted herself to what, she was forced to admit, seemed to be the inscrutable will of God for the discipline and humiliation of the Church. In a sort of bewildered resignation she waited to see what further sufferings were to come, to fill up the measure of the punishment which, for some mysterious purpose, the faithful must endure. But when close upon all this discomfiture and humiliation of her Church followed the discomfiture and humiliation of her country in war, and the near and evident danger of an English-speaking people's possessing the land, all the smothered fire of the Señora's nature broke out afresh. With unfaltering hands she buckled on her husband's sword, and with dry eyes saw him go forth to fight. She had but one regret, that she was not the mother of sons to fight also.

"Would thou wert a man, Felipe," she exclaimed again and again in tones the child never forgot. "Would thou wert a man, that thou might go also to fight these foreigners!"

Any race under the sun would have been to the Señora less hateful than the American. She had scorned them in her girlhood, when they came trading to post after post. She scorned them still. The idea of being forced to wage a war with pedlers was to her too monstrous to be believed. In the outset she had no doubt that the Mexicans would win in the contest.

"What!" she cried, "shall we who won independence from Spain, be beaten by these traders? It is impossible!"

When her husband was brought home to her dead, killed in the last fight the Mexican forces made, she said icily, "He would have chosen to die rather than to have been forced to see his country in the hands of the enemy." And she was almost frightened at herself to see how this thought, as it dwelt in her mind, slew the grief in her heart. She had believed she could not live if her husband were to be taken away from her; but she found herself often glad that he was dead,— glad that he was spared the sight and the knowledge of the things which happened; and even the yearning tenderness with which her imagination pictured him among the saints, was often turned into a fierce wondering whether indignation did not fill his soul, even in heaven, at the way things were going in the land for whose sake he had died.

Out of such throes as these had been born the second nature which made Señora Moreno the silent, reserved, stern, implacable woman they knew, who knew her first when she was sixty. Of the gay, tender, sentimental girl, who danced and laughed with the officers, and prayed and confessed with the Fathers, forty years before, there was small trace left now, in the low-voiced, white-haired, aged woman, silent, unsmiling, placid-faced, who manoeuvred with her son and her head shepherd alike, to bring it about that a handful of Indians might once more confess their sins to a Franciscan monk in the Moreno chapel.

1884

NATHANAEL WEST

The Day of the Locust

AROUND QUITTING time, Tod Hackett heard a
great din on the road outside his office. The groan of leather mingled
with the jangle of iron and over all beat the tattoo of a thousand
hooves. He hurried to the window.

An army of cavalry and foot was passing. It moved like a mob;
its lines broken, as though fleeing from some terrible defeat. The
dolmans of the hussars, the heavy shakos of the guards, Hanoverian
light horse, with their flat leather caps and flowing red plumes, were
all jumbled together in bobbing disorder. Behind the cavalry came the
infantry, a wild sea of waving sabretaches, sloped muskets, crossed
shoulder belts and swinging cartridge boxes. Tod recognized the
scarlet infantry of England with their white shoulder pads, the black
infantry of the Duke of Brunswick, the French grenadiers with their
enormous white gaiters, the Scotch with bare knees under plaid skirts.

While he watched, a little fat man, wearing a cork sun-helmet,
polo shirt and knickers, darted around the corner of the building in
pursuit of the army.

"Stage Nine—you bastards—Stage Nine!" he screamed through a
small megaphone.

The cavalry put spur to their horses and the infantry broke into
a dogtrot. The little man in the cork hat ran after them, shaking his
fist and cursing.

Tod watched until they had disappeared, behind half a Missis-
sippi steamboat, then put away his pencils and drawing board, and left
the office. On the sidewalk outside the studio he stood for a moment
trying to decide whether to walk home or take a streetcar. He had
been in Hollywood less than three months and still found it a very
exciting place, but he was lazy and didn't like to walk. He decided to
take the streetcar as far as Vine Street and walk the rest of the way.

A talent scout for National Films had brought Tod to the Coast after seeing some of his drawings in an exhibit of undergraduate work at the Yale School of Fine Arts. He had been hired by telegram. If the scout had met Tod, he probably wouldn't have sent him to Hollywood to learn set and costume designing. His large sprawling body, his slow blue eyes and sloppy grin made him seem completely without talent, almost doltish in fact.

Yes, despite his appearance, he was really a very complicated young man with a whole set of personalities, one inside the other like a nest of Chinese boxes. And "The Burning of Los Angeles," a picture he was soon to paint, definitely proved he had talent.

He left the car at Vine Street. As he walked along, he examined the evening crowd. A great many of the people wore sports clothes which were not really sports clothes. Their sweaters, knickers, slacks, blue flannel jackets with brass buttons were fancy dress. The fat lady in the yachting cap was going shopping, not boating; the man in the Norfolk jacket and Tyrolean hat was returning, not from a mountain, but an insurance office; and the girl in slacks and sneaks with a bandanna around her head had just left a switchboard, not a tennis court.

Scattered among these masquerades were people of a different type. Their clothing was somber and badly cut, brought from mail-order houses. While the others moved rapidly, darting into stores and cocktail bars, they loitered on the corners or stood with their backs to the shop windows and stared at everyone who passed. When their stare was returned, their eyes filled with hatred. At this time Tod knew very little about them except that they had come to California to die.

He was determined to learn much more. They were the people he felt he must paint. He would never again do a fat red barn, old stone wall or sturdy Nantucket fisherman. From the moment he had seen them, he had known that, despite his race, training and heritage, neither Winslow Homer nor Thomas Ryder could be his masters and he turned to Goya and Daumier.

He had learned this just in time. During his last year in art school, he had begun to think that he might give up painting completely. The pleasures he received from the problems of composition and color had decreased as his facility had increased and he had realized that he was going the way of all his classmates, toward illustration or mere handsomeness. When the Hollywood job had come along, he had grabbed it despite the arguments of his friends who were certain that he was selling out and would never paint again.

He reached the end of Vine Street and began the climb into Pinyon Canyon. Night had started to fall.

The edges of the trees burned with a pale violet light and their centers gradually turned from deep purple to black. The same violet piping, like the Neon tube, outlined the tops of the ugly, hump-backed hills and they were almost beautiful.

But not even the soft wash of dusk could help the houses. Only dynamite would be of any use against the Mexican ranch houses, Samoan huts, Mediterranean villas, Egyptian and Japanese temples, Swiss chalets, Tudor cottages, and every possible combination of these styles that lined the slopes of the canyon.

When he noticed that they were all of plaster, lath and paper, he was charitable and blamed their shape on the materials used. Steel, stone and brick curb a builder's fancy a little, forcing him to distribute his stresses and weights and to keep his corners plumb, but plaster and paper know no law, not even that of gravity.

On the corner of La Huerta Road was a miniature Rhine castle with tarpaper turrets pierced for archers. Next to it was a highly colored shack with domes and minarets out of the *Arabian Nights.* Again he was charitable. Both houses were comic, but he didn't laugh. Their desire to startle was so eager and guileless.

It is hard to laugh at the need for beauty and romance, no matter how tasteless, even horrible, the results of that are. But it is easy to sigh. Few things are sadder than the truly monstrous.

When Tod reached the street, he saw a dozen great violet shafts of light moving across the evening sky in wide crazy sweeps. Whenever one of the fiery columns reached the lowest point of its arc, it lit for a moment the rose-colored domes and delicate minarets of Kahn's Persian Palace Theatre. The purpose of this display was to signal the world premiere of a new picture.

Turning his back on the searchlights, he started in the opposite direction, toward Homer's place. Before he had gone very far, he saw a clock that read a quarter past six and changed his mind about going back just yet. He might as well let the poor fellow sleep for another hour and kill some time by looking at the crowds.

When still a block from the theatre, he saw an enormous electric sign that hung over the middle of the street. In letters ten feet high he read that—

"MR. KAHN A PLEASURE DOME DECREED"

Although it was still several hours before the celebrities would arrive, thousands of people had already gathered. They stood facing the theatre with their backs toward the gutter in a thick line hundreds of feet long. A big squad of policemen was trying to keep a lane open between the front rank of the crowd and the façade of the theatre.

Tod entered the lane while the policeman guarding it was busy with a woman whose parcel had torn open, dropping oranges all over the place. Another policeman shouted for him to get the hell across the street, but he took a chance and kept going. They had enough to do without chasing him. He noticed how worried they looked and how careful they tried to be. If they had to arrest someone, they joked good-naturedly with the culprit, making light of it until they got him around the corner, then they whaled him with their clubs. Only so long as the man was actually part of the crowd did they have to be gentle.

Tod had walked only a short distance along the narrow lane when he began to get frightened. People shouted, commenting on his hat, his carriage, and his clothing. There was a continuous roar of catcalls, laughter and yells, pierced occasionally by a scream. The scream was usually followed by a sudden movement in the dense mass and part of it would surge forward wherever the police line was weakest. As soon as that part was rammed back, the bulge would pop out somewhere else.

The police force would have to be doubled when the stars started to arrive. At the sight of their heroes and heroines, the crowd would turn demoniac. Some little gesture, either too pleasing or too offensive, would start it moving and then nothing but machine guns would stop it. Individually the purpose of its members might simply to be to get a souvenir, but collectively it would grab and rend.

A young man with a portable microphone was describing the scene. His rapid, hysterical voice was like that of a revivalist preacher whipping his congregation toward the ecstasy of fits.

"What a crowd, folks! What a crowd! There must be ten thousand excited, screaming fans outside Kahn's Persian tonight. The police can't hold them. Here, listen to them roar."

He held the microphone out and those near it obligingly roared for him.

"Did you hear it? It's a bedlam, folks. A veritable bedlam! What excitement! Of all the premières I've attended, this is the most . . . the most . . . stupendous, folks. Can the police hold them? Can they? It doesn't look so, folks . . . "

Another squad of police came charging up. The sergeant pleaded with the announcer to stand further back so the people couldn't hear him. His men threw themselves at the crowd. It allowed itself to be hustled and shoved out of habit and because it lacked an objective. It tolerated the police, just as a bull elephant does when he allows a small boy to drive him with a light stick.

Tod could see very few people who looked tough, nor could he see any working men. The crowd was made up of the lower middle classes, every other person one of his torchbearers.

Just as he came near the end of the lane, it closed in front of him with a heave, and he had to fight his way through. Someone knocked his hat off and when he stooped to pick it up, someone kicked him. He whirled around angrily and found himself surrounded by people who were laughing at him. He knew enough to laugh with them. The crowd became sympathetic. A stout woman slapped him on the back, while a man handed him his hat, first brushing it carefully with his sleeve. Still another man shouted for a way to be cleared.

By a great deal of pushing and squirming, always trying to look as though he were enjoying himself, Tod finally managed to break into the open. After rearranging his clothes, he went over to a parking lot and sat down on the low retaining wall that ran along the front of it.

New groups, whole families, kept arriving. He could see a change come over them as soon as they had become part of the crowd. Until they reached the line, they looked diffident, almost furtive, but the moment they had become part of it, they turned arrogant and pugnacious. It was a mistake to think them harmless curiosity seekers. They were savage and bitter, especially the middle-aged and the old, and had been made so by boredom and disappointment.

All their lives they had slaved at some kind of dull, heavy labor, behind desks and counters, in the fields and at tedious machines of all sorts, saving their pennies and dreaming of the leisure that would be theirs when they had enough. Finally that day came. They could draw a weekly income of ten or fifteen dollars. Where else should they go but California, the land of sunshine and oranges?

Once there, they discover that sunshine isn't enough. They get tired of oranges, even of avocado pears and passion fruit. Nothing happens. They don't know what to do with their time. They haven't the mental equipment for leisure, the money nor the physical equipment for pleasure. Did they slave so long just to go to an occasional Iowa picnic? What else is there? They watch the waves come in at Venice. There wasn't any ocean where most of them came from, but after you've seen one wave, you've seen them all. The same is true of the airplanes at Glendale. If only a plane would crash once in a while so that they could watch the passengers being consumed in a "holocaust of flame," as the newspapers put it. But the planes never crash.

Their boredom becomes more and more terrible. They realize that they've been tricked and burn with resentment. Every day of their lives they read the newspapers and went to the movies. Both fed them on lynchings, murder, sex crimes, explosions, wrecks, love nests, fires, miracles, revolutions, wars. This daily diet made sophisticates of them. The sun is a joke. Oranges can't titillate their jaded palates. Nothing can ever be violent enough to make taut their slack minds and bodies. They have been cheated and betrayed. They have slaved and saved for nothing.

Tod stood up. During the ten minutes he had been sitting on the wall, the crowd had grown thirty feet and he was afraid that his escape might be cut off if he loitered much longer. He crossed to the other side of the street and started back.

1939

JACK WEBB

The Badge

I

THE PAMPHLET given visitors to Los Angeles says the City Hall stands just about at the geographical center of the city. On a clear day, if you ride the elevator some 450 feet to the observation tower, you see a mass of concrete, granite, timber and just plain rock—one of the strangest, most picturesque and complicated police beats in the world.

You look north fifteen miles to Mount Wilson in the Sierra Madres, west thirteen miles to Venice and the Pacific. To the northwest, Hollywood seems to huddle against the Santa Monica mountains, and twenty miles south lies the harbor, the biggest man-made port in the world. East and southeast stretch the city's major industrial areas.

Here is a sprawling, magnetic, fantastic city whose feet rest on the sand at sea level and whose shoulders proudly rise to a mountain almost a mile high. Along coastline, mountain pass and desert flatland, you can ride its twisting perimeter for 312 miles. North to south, there are forty-four miles in which to hide a body. East to west, twenty-five miles in which to rob, plunder, attack.

Once a sleepy pueblo, now crowding the top in U.S. population, Los Angeles has attracted all manner of men, vice, and crime. Among its 2,500,000 inhabitants, the daily collision of good and bad, hunter and victim, passes reckoning. While the homicide detective is investigating a rape near the beach, the robbery detective is busy with a supermarket stickup in the San Fernando Valley.

And in between, in the score of individual communities, in any of the one million dwellings, no one knows—no one can know—what other evil is being planned, or already taking place.

Once Los Angeles was the capital of glamour, and then the movie studios began to disperse and sometimes disappear. Then the aircraft plant, the rubber factory, and the automobile assembly line elbowed in. Once the Mexicans and Chinese flooded the city, but the pioneer from back East, today as well as one hundred years ago, has staked his claim here, too.

Since no influence vanishes entirely, there is a residue of elegant sin and two-bit robberies, fantan and poker, calculated crime and impetuous knifing. The Angeleno will travel half a day to spend thirty minutes admiring desert flowers or lunching in a native sycamore grove. In his unpredictable way, he also will step across the line and commit a crime that is as grotesque as anything that comes out of Place Pigalle.

Against the danger, the police in the largest incorporated city in the United States have a dozen geographical enforcement divisions and dozens of specialists in every crime from bunco to murder. But unlike most federal police agencies, which are charged with enforcing specific laws, LAPD must be a housekeeper of all crime.

While the beach rape and the supermarket stickup are under investigation, traffic must flow freely during rush hour; and if a child strays from home, the patrolman on the beat takes time out to return him. Most of the work is far from spectacular, and often the spectacular is not successful.

For every individual, mostly Angelenos, who remember LAPD triumphs, there are a thousand who remember a Los Angeles woman killing: The Black Dahlia murder. That is, so to speak, the other side of the shield.

II

She was a lazy girl and irresponsible; and, when she chose to work, she drifted obscurely from one menial job to another, in New England, south to Florida, westward to the Coast.

No matter how they die, most drifters leave nothing behind, and many of the 25,000 graves dug yearly in Los Angeles are marked by blank stones, for their occupants didn't even leave a name. Yet today, more than a decade after her strange and awful death, this girl remains hauntingly, pathetically alive to many persons.

To the sociologist, she is the typical, unfortunate depression child who matured too suddenly in her teens into the easy money, easy living, easy loving of wartime America. To the criminologist, though the case is almost too melodramatic in its twists, her tortured, severed body is an eerie blend of Poe and Freud. To millions of plain Americans, fascinated by the combined savagery and cool intellect that went into her murder, she is "The Black Dahlia."

The other side of the shield.

Right from the first erroneous report to the police at 10:35 A.M. that gray mid-January day in 1947, the investigation was askew through no fault of the police. In the days, months, years of sleuthing that followed, it never quite got back into balance, again through no fault of the detectives. More than any other crime, murder is sometimes like that.

In the University section, along a dreary, weedy block without a house on either side, a housewife was walking to the store with her five-year-old daughter, scolding her a little because she wanted to play in the dew-wet lots.

Halfway up the block, the mother stopped in horror at something she saw in one of the lots. "What's that?" the child asked. The mother didn't answer. Grabbing her hand, she ran with her to the nearest neighbor's house to call the police.

And the first, wrong alarm went out: "Man down, 39th and Norton."

Within ten minutes, about 10:45 A.M., the first patrol car had reached the scene. Quickly a team of detectives from Central Division, a full crew from the Crime Lab, newspaper legmen, and photographers followed. The street was blocked off to keep back the curious, and the investigation got underway.

Sergeant Finis Arthur Brown of the Homicide Division, who was going to live with this ugly thing for months and years, hadn't yet arrived.

At 9 A.M. that day, he had been in court to testify in another case. After that, he went to Sixth and Rampart Streets to check out a dead-body report. An elderly man had died of natural causes, but Brown followed through with routine questioning of the rooming house operator.

Then there was a phone call for him. Captain Jack Donahoe told him to get over quick to the 3900 block on South Norton. "Looks like we got a bad one, Brownie," he warned.

At 11:05 A.M., just half an hour after the discovery of the body, Brown was there. He saw what he was up against, and, in another twenty-five minutes, additional manpower was at the scene. Nobody could say later that LAPD hadn't rolled hard and fast on this one.

Efficiently, detectives fanned out through the neighborhood. They wanted to find the woman who had made the first call. They hoped to locate some resident who had perhaps heard or seen something, *anything,* though the chances were one-hundred-to-one against them. The lot was a good hundred yards from the nearest house, and the body had probably been dumped at three or four o'clock in the morning.

They got nowhere. Neither did the "hard facts" men who sifted patiently through the weeds, turning up broken glass, rusted cans and other rubbish; but not a clue. The only bit of physical evidence was a set of tire marks on the pavement; and, if they came from the killer's car, they were never to prove useful.

But there was the body.

Old homicide hand though he was, Sergeant Brown had to make a conscious effort to study it.

It was nude. It showed evidence of slow, deliberate torture. There were neat, deep slashes around the breasts and on them. Rope burns on the wrists and ankles indicated the victim had been spread-eagled to heighten her agony. Her mouth had been deeply gashed from ear to ear so that her face was fixed in a grotesque and leering death smile. Finally, the body has been cleanly, surgically cut in two at the waist.

Brown was glad to turn away and check with Lee Jones of the Crime Lab. There were two interesting things to note. A sprinkling of bristles on the body indicated that it had been scrubbed. And, despite the lavish mutilation, there was only one drop of blood in the field.

Scientists, especially hard-bitten police scientists, usually don't give in to emotion. Lee Jones couldn't restrain himself. "This is the worst crime upon a woman I've ever seen," he blurted.

Sergeant Brown's pressing job was identification. But the body had been stripped, and there was only the long shot that maybe the girl had got into trouble and maybe her fingerprints were on file. Brown had copies of them rushed to the FBI in Washington by means of newspaper telephoto equipment.

Then he used the press another way, asking them to publish an artist's recreation of the girl's face (without the awful death smile). And, though not for publication, he had every inch of the weedy lot photographed, right down to three-dimensional shots of the severed corpse.

No one came forward to identify the victim, and though the forlorn files in Missing Persons were checked and rechecked, not a single description resembled the butchered remains at 39th and Norton.

But even before they knew whom they were looking for, LAPD launched the biggest crime hunt in modern Los Angeles history.

Every one of the city's dozen police divisions was subdivided down to each radio car beat. House to house, door to door in the apartment buildings, more than 250 policemen rang bells and asked questions.

Did you hear any unusual noises or screams last night or yesterday or the night before?

Have you noticed anything unusual around the neighborhood? Anybody acting peculiarly? Anybody digging in a yard, maybe buring a pile of woman's clothing? Or burning anything?

Very possibly, one of the 250 officers talked to the killer that day, or to someone who had a terrible suspicion about his (or her) identity. Yet all 250 drew a blank. Where the girl had been murdered was as much a mystery as the why of it, and the who, for that matter.

Next day the FBI kick-back supplied the who. Her name: Elizabeth Short, age 22; height, five feet five inches; weight, 120 pounds; race, Caucasian; sex, female; description, black hair (dyed) and blue eyes.

The FBI had her because just once, four years earlier in Santa Barbara, Elizabeth had been picked up. She was a minor then, and a policewoman caught her drinking in a bar with a girl friend and two soldiers. In a sense, it was ironic. The wrong way of life that was to lead her to death at least had left behind a clue to her identity, and she would escape the drifter's nameless grave.

Now that Brown had something to go on, the pace of the investigation accelerated. Who was Elizabeth Short? Where did she come from? What did she do? Boy friends? Associates? Habits? When was she last seen alive?

For seventy-two hours, Brown and many of the original twenty detectives assigned to the mystery worked day and night without letup. In fact, during the next thirty days, Brown was to cram in an additional thirty-three days of overtime. During one three-day period, he never got around to changing his shirt.

At the end of the first, furious three days of investigation, Brown knew a great deal about Betty Short or "The Black Dahlia," as an imaginative police reporter had re-christened her for all time. Those seventy-two hours had yielded the secret of The Dahlia's past right down to the date of her disappearance. Another seventy-two hours of such detective work, at most a week, and by all the normal odds LAPD would be putting the collar on a suspect.

Four years later, Sergeant Brown was down in Texas, chasing still another lead that lead nowhere.

The girl who was to bloom into the night flower was one of four sisters reared by their mother in Salem, Massachusetts. About the time the war broke out, when she was in her middle teens, Betty Short went to work. She ushered in theaters, she slung plates as a waitress. It was the kind of work where a girl too young and attractive would meet too many men.

For a time, her father reappeared in Salem, and then left again for northern California. Maybe there was something romantic about this man who came and went; maybe he told her stories about sunny California, so different from cold little Salem. At any rate, at eighteen, Betty went West and joined him briefly.

Then she struck out on her own for Los Angeles, the city of opportunity where many another waitress, poor but beautiful, had made it in the movies. She settled near the campus of the University of Southern California, and she may even have walked past the lot at 39th and Norton. It wasn't far away.

Los Angeles, like every other city, was at war. On a tip from a soldier, Betty went to Camp Cook, north of Los Angeles, and got a sales job in the PX.

Then the first ominous thing happened. Betty suddenly threw

up the job. There were barracks room whispers that some soldier had beaten her up badly. Why? Nobody seemed to know.

Betty drifted on to Santa Barbara; and, after the policewoman caught her in the bar with the two soldiers, she returned to New England. For almost two years, she sort of settled down, working as a waitress and cashier in a Boston restaurant.

Restlessness seized her again, and she took a bus all the way to Miami, working there for a winter. Then she came back to Boston and got a job across the Charles River in Cambridge in a café near the Harvard University campus.

There was a brief romance with a Harvard undergrad. All spring they dated; they even exchanged photographs. But when the school year ended in June, he went home; and Betty was on the move again. For a time, she lived in Indianapolis, and then in Chicago in the bright and noisy hotels that cluster round the Loop.

Something happened there that never has been fully established. Apparently, she met a handsome young Air Force flier. Maybe she even married him. No one has been able to check it out definitely, one way or the other.

At any rate, she loved him enough to go halfway across the country when he pleaded with her by wire to join him in Long Beach, California. There he met her at the train and took her to a hotel room he had arranged. From there, they journeyed on to Hollywood.

And then one day he told her he had to fly East to be separated from the service. He was like her college student; she never saw him again.

The war was over, the men were going home. At twenty-one, when she should have been starting married life or maybe a modest career, she was already obsolescent.

For three months, The Dahlia moved in with a girl friend; then went to a small home for would-be actresses; moved again to a private home; then to a hotel for girls in Hollywood.

She had no job. She killed time hanging around the radio studios and attending the radio shows. She sponged off friends and even got money from her mother back home. She lost her clothes to the landlady in lieu of rent. She mooched at the night spots and the bars where a pretty girl could easily cadge a drink. She was careless about the company she kept.

Two or three times, friends later remembered, Betty had hitched rides to the Sixth Street area when she was out of funds. After a day or so, she would reappear, mysteriously replenished. Where she got the money never was known.

Some six weeks before the end, The Dahlia met a salesman in Hollywood. The salesman rented a room for her in a hotel, but he signed the register "Mr. and Mrs." Later, he took her to a bus depot, bought her a ticket for San Diego and said good-bye.

In San Diego, aimless, drifting, The Dahlia happened into an all-night theater. She got into a conversation with the cashier. Little by little, The Dahlia let drop her affecting story of misfortune and unhappiness.

Generously, the cashier brought her home with her that night and then let her stay for the next month. But something seemed to be driving The Dahlia toward her fate. She met another young salesman and begged him to drive her to Los Angeles the following day.

Perhaps with romantic hopes in mind, he did so, but as soon as they arrived, The Dahlia skillfully avoided a dinner date with him. She had some other plan in mind. Her sister, she explained, was down from Berkeley and stopping at the Hotel Biltmore. Regretfully, the salesman waited while she checked her bag at the bus depot and then dropped her off at the hotel.

It was 7 P.M., January 10.

For three more hours, The Dahlia moved freely. Three hours in which chance, a friend happening by, or an attractive well-dressed stranger might have diverted her from her plan, whatever it was.

Dozens of men must have observed her, for she spent the time waiting near the phone booths and she was, in her black cardigan jacket and skirt, white blouse, red shoes, red purse, and beige sport coat, the kind of girl that men observe. Yet none offered a merciful, life-saving flirtation.

Once The Dahlia changed a dollar bill at the hotel cigar stand and made a phone call, maybe two. Then she waited, as though expecting a call back. When none came, she walked out the front door, smiling to the doorman as he tipped his cap. He observed her trim form swinging south on Olive Street toward Sixth, the slim legs striding easily, the red heels tapping purposefully on the sidewalk.

It was 10 P.M.

And thus Sergeant Brown traced The Dahlia back to childhood, forward to the brink of eternity. And there the investigation stood still. Five days, from the doorman's last salute to the living, up to the discovery of the mutilated thing, remained a blank.

Medical evidence could say what must have happened during part of that time, but not why or by whom, nor could it locate the abattoir.

The Dahlia had been roped and spread-eagled and then hour after hour, for possibly two or three days, slowly tortured with the little knife thrusts that hurt terribly but wouldn't kill. She had made the rope burns on her wrists and ankles as she writhed in agony.

Finally, in hot rage or *coup de grâce*, there had come the slash across the face from ear to ear, and The Dahlia choked to death on her own blood.

But the killer had not done with her body.

Afterwards, he (or she) drained the system of blood, scrubbed the body clean and even shampooed the hair. Then it was neatly cut in two and deposited at 39th and Norton.

Five days after the first report of "man down," the twenty original investigators were increased to fifty. Now the newspapers were playing the case as no crime had ever been played in Los Angeles, and the publicity was both a blessing and a burden to LAPD.

Every hour seemed to turn up a new "lead" that had to be checked out; and suddenly dozens of persons who had not recognized The Black Dahlia's sketch in the papers four days earlier volunteered bits and pieces of information about her life. Nothing, however trivial, could be ignored. Everything was run down, saved or discarded.

Some fifteen times, the Crime Lab and men from the Detective Bureau went over houses, from cellar to attic, where the slow torture killing might have been played out. They found nothing. Having been lost en route, The Dahlia's trunk at last arrived from Chicago. Again, nothing.

There had to be a touch of lunacy in a killing like that, and madness communicates with madness. Now the "confessions" began pouring in to irritate and distract Finis Brown. One man telephoned that he was coming in to surrender, and he did—three or four times when the detectives wouldn's believe him the first time. "Confessin' Tom," they finally called the nuisance.

At Fort Dix, New Jersey, a soldier sobbed out the story of the murder he hadn't committed. Four times at his own expense, a man traveled west from Utah and sat, drenched with sweat in the interrogation room, while he begged detectives to believe his preposterous admission of the killing.

At times it seemed the case needed a division psychiatrist more than a Homicide man, but with remarkable restraint, LAPD booked only one of the confessers for insanity.

In all, thirty-eight confessions had to be double-checked, and the waste of time was deplorable. Scores more had to be at least listened to before detectives knew they weren't worth even a rundown. Now and then, fighting to unclutter his few hard facts from all the fancies being pressed on him, Finis Brown wondered if he wouldn't tip over himself.

But if a madman had killed The Dahlia, he might be among those psychos, and the loony bin had to be emptied, one poor deluded mind at a time, just to make sure.

Then there were the stacks of mail that came in daily, mostly abusive, obscene or plain crazy but now and then intelligently written notes that were even more annoying. These contained pompous advice from amateur detectives telling the police how to go about their business.

Everything had to be read because The Dahlia's butcher might just be the egocentric who would delight in needling the police. At first, Sergeant Brown kept a ledger to catalogue the mail, but the volume overwhelmed him. So names and addresses of the writers were filed on cards to be checked out gradually when there was time for it.

In ten days, the hysteria seemed to have run its course. For the first time, the newspapers took The Dahlia off page one, and LAPD enjoyed a moment of quiet. The quiet before the storm, as it turned out.

That very same evening, a mail truck emptied a box near the Hotel Biltmore, and among other pieces picked up a simple carton, wrapped in brown paper and addressed to the police. Next morning, when they unwrapped the package, Finis Brown and his detectives relieved themselves with words that would have made an old Army sergeant shake his head in envy.

Inside were The Black Dahlia's purse, her Social Security card, her birth certificate, a batch of miscellaneous cards and papers, scraps with numbers and names on them, even an address book. The killer was laughing at Homicide, telling the detectives contemptuously to go ahead and make something of it.

But he (or she) had been careful to leave no traces. Postmark and printing, carton and brown paper, yielded no clues. There was a faint odor to the contents, and scientific tests confirmed the suspicions of the detectives. Everything had been carefully washed in gasoline to remove any trace of where it had been or who had touched it. Tantalizingly, about a hundred pages had been ripped out of the address book. Some two hundred names remained, and Finis Brown had each one checked out, in vain.

With this mocking gesture, the killer bowed out; and, though the papers hastily brought The Dahlia back to page one, though the humiliated detectives bird-dogged even harder, this was really the end of the line.

There is no statute of limitations on murder, and LAPD will not admit defeat.

Two years later, Finis Brown thought he had a lead on the mysterious soldier who had given Betty the bad beating at Camp Cook. The lead ran dry.

Three years later, he was able to make a complete check on the salesman who had signed the register "Mr. and Mrs." in Hollywood and then put her on the bus to San Diego.

Four years later, he was down in Austin and Dallas, Texas, and after that up in Boston interviewing the Harvard man who had dated her one spring.

Nothing, nothing, except to close out false scents and then try to get back to the right one.

Sometimes police know their man and yet cannot pin the evidence on him. Sometimes they sense with the hunter's intuition that they are close, very close, and lose him only because he has suddenly died or managed to flee into obscurity. Usually, almost always, they can reconstruct the motive and sex of the killer. Murder is their business, and these things are not surprising.

But with the monster who slowly, delectably tortured The Black Dahlia to death, they have never felt that they were anywhere near close. They have never known the motive, nor whether the slayer was man or woman, nor where the agony was perpetrated.

Was the killer The Dahlia's lover or husband who felt he had been betrayed? But what betrayal, even unfaithfulness or a mocking laugh, merited revenge like this?

Was it perhaps a woman who had taken The Dahlia as wife in Lesbian marriage? Was that why the body had to be bisected, so that she could carry out the parts to her car?

Was the killer, man or woman, a sadist with a blood fetish who slashed for no comprehensible reason at all?

All LAPD can say is that its detectives have exonerated every man and woman whom they've talked to, including the scores who insist to this day that they are guilty.

Beyond that, you are free to speculate. But do him a favor—don't press your deductions on Finis Brown.

III

Per capita, police protection costs you less than four cents a day in Los Angeles. Even for a year, the police bill of the average family is less than the gas bill for one month.

Is it worth it?

In sixteen months, LAPD managed to catch Donald Keith Bashor, who had killed Karil Graham and Laura Lindsay and terrorized the women of Westlake. In more than a decade, LAPD has, at enormous expense, made no progress in the Black Dahlia murder.

You've got to have policemen but are they worth $35 millions a year, twenty per cent of the whole Los Angeles budget?

Of course, if the gun is in *your* back, four cents, even $35 millions, is tragically insufficient. You don't count your life in those terms.

And if you're a cop, with better than any civilian's chance of catching a slug, you don't count your life in those terms, either. Something more than take-home pay is involved, and you don't like it when you're a hero today, a bum tomorrow.

With fewer policemen than it had only a few years ago, LAPD is making more arrests these days. A quarter of a million yearly, but just let the department blow a spectacular one and listen to the howls. "Dump cop," "flatfoot," "stupid."

THE BADGE . . . how do you judge the men who wear it—LAPD, any department, your police force in your town?

Headlines don't tell the story and neither do statistics though they are part of the yardstick. The system and the way it operates is part of the yardstick, too. So are the scientific facilities and the physical equipment, right down to good, grooved rubber on the wheels of speeding patrol units.

It helps to have a bright, honest chief; and it's no drawback if the commissioners who backstop him and the whole department are dedicated men. In the complicated modern business of criminology, there are a dozen complicated reasons for the success or failure of a police department.

But, mostly, these reasons boil down to two: the man in uniform and the civilian in mufti. If the peace officer is good, if the public supports him *and he knows it,* you have an honest department with polish and morale.

Unfortunately, too many of us dismiss crime and cops as an exotic something we read about in the newspapers. Maybe the kid's bike was stolen once, or there was a sneak theft of the milk money; but *real* crime, forgeries, sex offenses, beatings, poison pen letters, and especially murder, is what happens to somebody else. It is part of the price of modern living, *four cents a day,* and nothing to concern ourselves about seriously.

"The grave danger in such an attitude is in its possible spread to the police," says Chief William H. Parker of LAPD. "If the police philosophy of this country ever becomes permeated with a laissez faire attitude, we are in serious trouble."

As a citizen, you owe it to yourself to know something about the police, their limitations as well as their triumphs. The easiest way to do it is to study the LAPD in action, for LAPD, scaled down to size, might be *your* department.

After all, it is your life, your property that they protect.

1958

RAYMOND CHANDLER

Writers in Hollywood

HOLLYWOOD IS easy to hate, easy to sneer at, easy to lampoon. Some of the best lampooning has been done by people who have never been through a studio gate, some of the best sneering by egocentic geniuses who departed huffily—not forgetting to collect their last pay check—leaving behind them nothing but the exquisite aroma of their personalities and a botched job for the tired hacks to clean up.

I hold no brief for Hollywood. I have worked there a little over two years, which is far from enough to make me an authority, but more than enough to make me feel pretty thoroughly bored. That should not be so. The making of a picture ought surely to be a rather fascinating adventure. It is not; it is an endless contention of tawdry egos, some of them powerful, almost all of them vociferous, and almost none of them capable of anything much more creative than credit-stealing and self-promotion.

Hollywood is a showman's paradise. But showmen make nothing; they exploit what someone else has made. The publisher and the play producer are showmen too; but they exploit what is already made. The showmen of Hollywood control the making—and thereby degrade it. For the basic art of motion pictures is the screenplay; it is fundamental, without it there is nothing. Everything derives from the screenplay, and most of that which derives is an applied skill which, however adept, is artistically not in the same class with the creation of a screenplay. But in Hollywood the screenplay is written by a salaried writer under the supervision of a producer—that is to say, by an employee without power of decision over the uses of his own craft, without ownership of it, and, however extravagantly paid, almost without honor for it.

I am not interested in why the Hollywood system exists or persists, nor in learning out of what bitter struggles for prestige it arose, nor in how much money it succeeds in making out of bad pictures. I am interested only in the fact that as a result of it there is no such thing as an art of the screenplay, and there never will be as long as the system lasts, for it is the essence of this system that it seeks to exploit a talent without permitting it the right to be a talent. It cannot be done; you can only destroy the talent, which is exactly what happens—when there is any to destroy.

Granted that there isn't much. Some chatty publisher (probably Bennett Cerf) remarked once that there are writers in Hollywood making two thousand dollars a week who haven't had an idea in ten years. He exaggerated—backwards: there are writers in Hollywood making two thousand a week who never had an idea in their lives, who have never written a photographable scene, who could not make two cents a word in the pulp market if their lives depended on it. Hollywood is full of such writers, although there are few at such high salaries. They are, to put it bluntly, a pretty dreary lot of hacks, and most of them know it, and they take their kicks and their salaries and try to be reasonably grateful to an industry which permits them to live much more opulently than they could live anywhere else.

And I have no doubt that most of them, also, would like to be much better writers than they are, would like to have force and integrity and imagination—enough of these to earn a decent living at some art of literature that has the dignity of a free profession. It will not happen to them, and there is not much reason why it should. If it ever could have happened, it will not happen now. For even the best of them (with a few rare exceptions) devote their entire time to work which has no more possibility of distinction than a Pekinese has of becoming a Great Dane: to asinine musicals about technicolor legs and the yowling of night-club singers; to "psychological" dramas with wooden plots, stock characters, and that persistent note of fuzzy earnestness which suggests the conversation of schoolgirls in puberty; to sprightly and sophisticated comedies (we hope) in which the gags are as stale as the attitudes, in which there is always a drink in every hand, a butler in every doorway, and a telephone on the edge of every bathtub; to historical epics in which the male actors look like female impersonators, and the lovely feminine star looks just a little too starry-eyed for a babe who has spent half her life swapping husbands; and last but not least, to those pictures of deep social import in which everybody is thoughtful and grown-up and sincere and the most difficult problems of life are wordily resolved into a unanimous vote of confidence in the inviolability of the Constitution, the sanctity of the home, and the paramount importance of the streamlined kitchen.

And these, dear readers, are the million-dollar babies—the cream of the crop. Most of the boys and girls who write for the screen never get anywhere near this far. They devote their sparkling lines and their structural finesse to horse operas, cheap gun-in-the-kidney melodramas, horror items about mad scientists and cliffhangers concerned with screaming blondes and circular saws. The writers of this tripe are licked before they start. Even in a purely technical sense their work is doomed for lack of the time to do it properly. The challenge of screenwriting is to say much in little and then take half of that little out and still preserve an effect of leisure and natural movement. Such a technique requires experiment and elimination. The cheap pictures simply cannot afford it.

Let me not imply that there are no writers of authentic ability in Hollywood. There are not many, but there are not many anywhere. The creative gift is a scarce commodity, and patience and imitation have always done most of its work. There is no reason to expect from the anonymous toilers of the screen a quality which we are very obviously not getting from the publicized litterateurs of the best-seller list, from the compilers of fourth-rate historical novels which sell half a million copies, from the Broadway candy butchers known as playwrights, or from the sulky maestri of the little magazines.

To me the interesting point about Hollywood's writers of talent is not how few or how many they are, but how little of worth their talent is allowed to achieve. Interesting—but hardly unexpected, once you accept the premise that writers are employed to write screenplays on the theory that, being writers, they have a particular gift and training for the job, and are then prevented from doing it with any independence or finality whatsoever, on the theory that, being merely writers, they know nothing about making pictures; and of course if they don't know how to make pictures, they couldn't possibly know how to write them. It takes a producer to tell them that.

I do not wish to become unduly vitriolic on the subject of producers. My own experience does not justify it, and after all, producers too are slaves of the system. Also, the term "producer" is of very vague definition. Some producers are powerful in their own right, and some are little more than legmen for the front office; some—few, I trust—receive less money than some of the writers who work for them. It is even said that in one large Hollywood studio there are producers who are lower than writers; not merely in earning power, but in prestige, importance, and aesthetic ability. It is, of course, a *very* large studio where all sorts of unexplained things could happen and hardly be noticed.

For my thesis the personal qualities of a producer are rather beside the point. Some are able and humane men and some are low-grade individuals with the morals of a goat, the artistic integrity of a slot machine, and the manners of a floorwalker with delusions of grandeur. In so far as the writing of the screenplay is concerned, however, the producer is the boss; the writer either gets along with him and his ideas (if he has any) or gets out. This means both personal and artistic subordination, and no writer of quality will long accept either without surrendering that which made him a writer of quality, without dulling the fine edge of his mind, without becoming little by little a conniver rather than a creator, a supple and facile journeyman rather than a craftsman of original thought.

It makes very little difference how a writer feels toward his producer as a man; the fact that the producer can change and destroy and disregard his work can only operate to diminish that work in its conception and make it mechanical and indifferent in execution. The impulse to perfection cannot exist where the definition of perfection is the arbitrary decision of authority. That which is born in loneliness and from the heart cannot be defended against the judgment of a committee of sycophants. The volatile essences which make literature cannot survive the clichés of a long series of story conferences. There is little magic of word or emotion or situation which can remain alive after the incessant bone-scraping revisions imposed on the Hollywood writer by the process of rule by decree. That these magics do somehow, here and there, by another and even rarer magic, survive and reach the screen more or less intact is the infrequent miracle which keeps Hollywood's handful of fine writers from cutting their throats.

Hollywood has no right to expect such miracles, and it does not deserve the men who bring them to pass. Its conception of what makes a good picture is still as juvenile as its treatment of writing talent is insulting and degrading. Its idea of "production value" is spending a million dollars dressing up a story that any good writer would throw away. Its vision of the rewarding movie is a vehicle for some glamorpuss with two expessions and eighteen changes of costume, or for some male idol of the muddled millions with a permanent hangover, six worn-out acting tricks, the build of a lifeguard, and the mentality of a chicken-strangler. Pictures for such purposes as these, Hollywood lovingly and carefully makes. The good ones smack it in the rear when it isn't looking.

There is no present indication whatever that the Hollywood writer is on the point of acquiring any real control over his work, any right to choose what that work shall be (other than refusing jobs, which he can only do within narrow limits), or even any right to decide how the values in the producer-chosen work shall be brought out. There is no present guarantee that his best lines, best ideas, best scenes will not be changed or omitted on the set by the director or dropped on the floor during the later process of cutting—for the simple but essential reason that the best things in any picture, artistically speaking, are invariably the easiest to leave out, mechanically speaking.

There is no attempt in Hollywood to exploit the writer as an artist of meaning to the picture-buying public; there is every attempt to keep the public uninformed about his vital contribution to whatever art the movie contains. On the billboards, in the newspaper advertisements, his name will be smaller than that of the most insignificant bit-player who achieves what is known as billing; it will be the first to disappear as the size of the ad is cut down toward the middle of the week; it will be the last and least to be mentioned in any word-of-mouth or radio promotion.

The first picture I worked on was nominated for an Academy award (if that means anything), but I was not even invited to the press review held right in the studio. An extremely successful picture made by another studio from a story I wrote used verbatim lines out of the story in its promotional campaign, but my name was never mentioned once in any radio, magazine, billboard, or newspaper advertising that I saw or heard—and I saw and heard a great deal. This neglect is of no consequence to me personally; to any writer of books a Hollywood by-line is trivial. To those whose whole work is in Hollywood it is not trivial, because it is part of a deliberate and successful plan to reduce the professional screenwriter to the status of an assistant picture-maker, superficially deferred to (while he is in the room), essentially ignored, and even in his most brilliant achievements carefully pushed out of the way of any possible accolade which might otherwise fall to the star, the producer, the director.

If all this is true, why then should any writer of genuine ability continue to work in Hollywood at all? The obvious reason is not enough: few screenwriters possess homes in Bel-Air, illuminated swimming pools, wives in full-length mink coats, three servants, and that air of tired genius gone a little sour. Money buys pathetically little in Hollywoood beyond the pleasure of living in an unreal world, associating with a narrow group of people who think, talk, and drink nothing but pictures, most of them bad, and the doubtful pleasure of watching famous actors and actresses guzzle in some of the rudest restaurants in the world.

I do not mean that Hollywood society is any duller or more dissipated than moneyed society anywhere: God knows it couldn't be. But it is a pretty thin reward for a lifetime devoted to the essential craft of what might be a great art. I suppose the truth is that the veterans of the Hollywood scene do not realize how little they are getting, how many dull egotists they have to smile at, how many shoddy people they have to treat as friends, how little real accomplishment is possible, how much gaudy trash their life contains. The superficial friendliness of Hollywood is pleasant—until you find out that nearly every sleeve conceals a knife. The companionship during working hours with men and women who take the business of fiction seriously gives a pale heat to the writer's lonely soul. It is so easy to forget that there is a world in which men buy their own groceries and, if they choose, think their own thoughts. In Hollywood you don't even write your own checks—and what you think is what you hope some producer or studio executive will like.

Beyond this I suppose there is hope; there are several hopes. The cold dynasty will not last forever, the dictatorial producer is already a little unsure, the top-heavy director has long since become a joke in his own studio; after a while even technicolor will not save him. There is hope that a decayed and makeshift system will pass, that somehow the flatulent moguls will learn that only writers can write screenplays and only proud and independent writers can write good screenplays, and that present methods of dealing with such men are destructive of the very force by which pictures must live.

And there is the intense and beautiful hope that the Hollywood writers themselves—such of them as are capable of it—will recognize that writing for the screen is no job for amateurs and half-writers whose problems are always solved by somebody else. It is the writers' own weakness as craftsmen that permits the superior egos to bleed them white of initiative, imagination, and integrity. If even a quarter of the *highly paid* screenwriters in Hollywood could produce a completely integrated and photographable screenplay under their own power, with only the amount of interference and discussion necessary to protect the studio's investment in actors and ensure a reasonable freedom from libel and censorship troubles, then the producer would assume his proper function of coördinating and conciliating the various crafts which combine to make a picture; and the director—heaven help his strutting soul—would be reduced to the ignominious task of making pictures as they are conceived and written—and not as the director would try to write them, if only he knew how to write.

Certainly there are producers and directors—although how pitifully few—who are sincere enough to want such a change, and talented enough to have no fear of its effect on their own position. Yet it is only a little over three years since the major (and only this very year the minor) studios were forced, after prolonged and bitter struggle, to agree to treat the writers according to some reasonable standard of business ethics.

This struggle is still going on; in a sense it will always go on, in a sense it always *should* go on. But so far the cards are stacked against the writer. If there is no art of the screenplay, the reason is at least partly that there exists no available body of technical theory and practice by which it can be learned. There is no available library of screenplay literature, because the screenplays belong to the studios, and they will only show them within their guarded walls. There is no body of critical opinion, because there are no critics of the screenplay; there are only critics of motion pictures as entertainment, and most of these critics know nothing whatever of the means whereby the motion picture is created and put on celluloid. There is no teaching, because there is no one to teach. If you do not know how pictures are made, you cannot speak with any authority on how they should be constructed; if you do, you are busy enough trying to do it.

There is no correlation of crafts within the studio itself; the average – and far better than average – screenwriter knows hardly anything of the technical problems of the director, and nothing at all of the superlative skill of the trained cutter. He spends his effort in writing shots that cannot be made, or which if made would be thrown away; in writing dialogue that cannot be spoken, sound effects that cannot be heard, and nuances of mood and emotion which the camera cannot reproduce. His idea of an effective scene is something that has to be shot down a stair well or out of a gopher hole; or a conversation so static that the director, in order to impart a sense of motion to it, is compelled to photograph it from nine different angles.

In fact, no part of the vast body of technical knowledge which Hollywood contains is systematically and as a matter of course made available to the new writer in a studio. They tell him to look at pictures – which is to learn architecture by staring at a house. And then they send him back to his rabbit hutch to write little scenes which his producer, in between telephone calls to his blondes and booze-companions, will tell him ought to have been written quite differently. The producer is probably correct; the scene ought to have been written differently. It ought to have been written right. But first it had to be written. The producer didn't do that. He wouldn't know how. Anyway he's too busy. And he's making too much money. And the atmosphere of intellectual squalor in which the salaried writer operates would offend his dignity.

I have kept the best hope of all for the last. In spite of all I have said, the writers of Hollywood *are* winning their battle for prestige. More and more of them are becoming showmen in their own right, producers and directors of their own screenplays. Let us be glad for their additional importance and power, and not examine the artistic result too critically. The boys make good (and some of them might even make good pictures). Let us rejoice together, for the tendency to become showmen is well in the acceptable tradition of the literary art as practiced among the cameras.

For the very nicest thing Hollywood can possibly think of to say to a writer is that he is too good to be only a writer.

1945

CHARLES BRACKETT, BILLY WILDER, AND D. M. MARSHMAN, JR.

Screenplay for *Sunset Boulevard*

S T A R T the picture with the actual street sign: SUNSET BOULEVARD, stencilled on a curbstone. In the gutter lie dead leaves, scraps of paper, burnt matches and cigarette butts. It is early morning.

Now the CAMERA leaves the sign and MOVES EAST, the grey asphalt of the street filling the screen. As speed accelerates to around 40 m.p.h., traffic demarcations, white arrows, speed-limit warnings, manhole covers, etc., flash by. SUPERIMPOSED on all of this are the CREDIT TITLES, in the stencilled style of the street sign.

> GILLIS
> Well, I drove down Sunset Boulevard one afternoon. That was my mistake . . . Maybe I'd better start off with the morning of that day. I've been out of work for six months . . .

Gillis' voice overlaps a SLOW DISSOLVE INTO:

Hollywood seen from the hilltop at Ivar & Franklin streets

In contrast to the eeriness of the morgue, everything is crisp and bright in the sunshine. Gillis' voice continues speaking as the CAMERA PANS toward the ALTO NIDO APARTMENT HOUSE, an ugly stucco Moorish structure, some four stories high. CAMERA MOVES TOWARD *an open window* on the third floor, and right into:

GILLIS' VOICE

I had a couple of stories out that wouldn't sell, and an apartment right above Hollywood and Ivar that wasn't paid for. Come to think of it, a lot of things weren't paid for—my car, my laundry, Dave, the delicatessen man . . . I was trying to pound out a western this time, but it was like pulling teeth. I was in a slump, all right.

Joe Gillis' Apartment

It is a one-room affair, with an unmade Murphy bed pulled out of the wall. There are a couple of worn-out plush chairs and a Spanish-style, wrought-iron standing lamp. Also a small desk littered with books and letters, and a chest of drawers with a portable phonograph and some records on top. On the walls are a couple of reproductions of characterless paintings, with laundry bills and snapshots stuck in the frames. Through an archway can be seen a tiny kitchenette, complete with unwashed coffee pot and cup, empty tin cans, orange peels, etc. The effect is dingy and cheerless—just another furnished apartment.

It is about noon. Joe Gillis, barefooted and wearing nothing except shorts and an old bathrobe, is sitting on the bed. In front of him, on a straight chair, is a portable typewriter. Beside him, on the bed, is a dirty ashtray and a scattering of typewritten and pencil-marked pages. Gillis is typing, with a pencil clenched between his teeth.

The buzzer SOUNDS.

GILLIS
Yeah.

The buzzer SOUNDS again. Gillis opens the door. Two men, wearing hats, are standing outside, one of them carrying a briefcase.

NO. 1
Joseph C. Gillis?

GILLIS
That's right.

The men ease into the room. No. 1 hands Gillis a business card.

NO. 1
We've come for the car.

GILLIS
What car?

NO. 2
(Consulting a paper) 1946 Plymouth convertible. California license 97 N 567.

NO. 1
Where are the keys?

GILLIS
Why should I give you the keys?

NO. 1
Because the company's played ball with you long enough. Because you're three payments behind. And because we've got a court order. Come on—the keys.

NO. 2
Or do you want us to jack it up and haul it away?

GILLIS
Relax, fans. The car isn't here.

NO. 1
Is that so?

GILLIS
I lent it to a friend of mine. He took it up to Palm Springs.

NO. 1
Had to get away for his health, I suppose.

GILLIS
You don't believe me? Look in the garage.

NO. 1

Sure we believe you, only now we want you to believe *us*. That car better be back here by noon tomorrow, or there's going to be fireworks.

GILLIS

You say the cutest things.

The men leave. Gillis stands pondering beside the door for a moment. Then he walks to the center of the room and, with his back to the CAMERA, slips into a pair of gray slacks. There is a metallic noise as some loose change and keys drop from the trouser pockets. As Gillis bends over to pick them up, we see that he has dropped the car keys, identifiable because of a rabbit's foot and a miniature license plate attached to the key-ring. Gillis pockets the keys and as he starts to put on a shirt

GILLIS' VOICE

Well, I needed about two hundred and ninety dollars and I needed it real quick, or I'd lose my car. It wasn't in Palm Springs and it wasn't in the garage. I was way ahead of the finance company.

DISSOLVE TO:

Exterior of Rudy's Shoeshine Parlor (day)

A small shack-like building, it stands in the corner of a public parking lot. Rudy, a colored boy, is giving a customer a shine.

GILLIS' VOICE

(continued) I knew they'd be coming around and I wasn't taking any chances, so I kept it a couple of blocks away in a parking lot behind Rudy's Shoeshine Parlor. Rudy never asked any questions. He'd just look at your heels and know the score.

PAN BEHIND the shack to *GILLIS' CAR*, a yellow 1946 Plymouth convertible with the top down. Gillis enters the SHOT. He is wearing a tweed sport jacket, a tan polo shirt, and moccasins. He steps into the car and drives it off. Rudy winks after him.

The alley next to Sidney's Men's Shop on Bronson Ave.

Gillis drives into the alley and parks his car right behind a delivery truck. PAN AND FOLLOW HIM as he gets out, walks around the corner into Bronson and then toward the towering main gate of Paramount. A few loafers, studio cops and extras are lounging there.

GILLIS' VOICE

I had an original story kicking around Paramount. My agent told me it was dead as a doornail, but I knew a big shot over there who'd always liked me, and then time had come to take a little advantage of it. His name was Sheldrake. He was a smart producer, with a set of ulcers to prove it.

DISSOLVE TO:

Sheldrake's office

It is in the style of a Paramount executive's office—mahogany, leather, and a little chintz. On the walls are some large framed photographs of Paramount stars, with dedications to Mr. Sheldrake. Also a couple of framed critics' awards certificates, and an Oscar on a bookshelf. A shooting schedule chart is thumb-tacked into a large bulletin board. There are piles of scripts, a few pipes and, somewhere in the background, some set models.

Start on Sheldrake. He is about 45. Behind his worried face there hides a coated tongue. He is engaged in changing the stained filter cigarette in his Zeus holder.

SHELDRAKE
All right, Gillis. You've got five minutes. What's your story about?

GILLIS
It's about a ball player, a rookie shortstop that's batting 347. The poor kid was once mixed up in a holdup. But he's trying to go straight—except there's a bunch of gamblers who won't let him.

SHELDRAKE
So they tell the kid to throw the World Series, or else, huh?

GILLIS

More or less. Only for the end I've got a gimmick that's real good.

A secretary enters, carrying a glass of milk. She opens a drawer and takes out a bottle of pills for Sheldrake.

SHELDRAKE

Got a title?

GILLIS

Bases Loaded. There's a 40-page outline.

SHELDRAKE

(To the secretary) Get the Readers' Department and see what they have on Bases Loaded.

The secretary exits. Sheldrake takes a pill and washes it down with some milk.

GILLIS

They're pretty hot about it over at Twentieth, but I think Zanuck's all wet. Can you see Ty Power as a shortstop? You've got the best man for it right here on this lot. Alan Ladd. Good change of pace for Alan Ladd. There's another thing: it's pretty simple to shoot. Lot of outdoor stuff. Bet you could make the whole thing for under a million. And there's a great little part for Bill Demarest. One of the trainers, an oldtime player who got beaned and goes out of his head sometimes.

The door opens and Betty Schaefer enters—a clean-cut, nice looking girl of 21, with a bright, alert manner. Dressed in tweed skirt, Brooks sweater and pearls, and carrying a folder of papers. She puts them on Sheldrake's desk, not noticing Gillis, who stands near the door.

BETTY

Hello, Mr. Sheldrake. On that Bases Loaded. I covered it with a 2-page synopsis.

(She holds it out) But I wouldn't bother.

SHELDRAKE
What's wrong with it?

BETTY
It's from hunger.

SHELDRAKE
Nothing for Ladd?

BETTY
Just a rehash of something that wasn't very good to begin with.

SHELDRAKE
I'm sure you'll be glad to meet Mr. Gillis. He wrote it.

Betty turns toward Gillis, embarrassed.

SHELDRAKE
This is Miss Kramer.

BETTY
Schaefer. Betty Schaefer. And right now I wish I could crawl into a hole and pull it in after me.

GILLIS
If I could be of any help . . .

BETTY
I'm sorry Mr. Gillis, but I just don't think it's any good. I found it flat and banal.

GILLIS
Exactly what kind of material do you recommend? James Joyce? Dostoevsky?

SHELDRAKE

Name dropper.

BETTY

I just think pictures should say a little something.

GILLIS

Oh, you're one of the message kids. Just a story won't do. You'd have turned down Gone With the Wind.

SHELDRAKE

No, that was me. I said, Who wants to see a Civil War picture?

BETTY

Perhaps the reason I hated Bases Loaded is that I knew your name: I'd always heard you had some talent.

GILLIS

That was last year. This year I'm trying to earn a living.

BETTY

So you take Plot 27-A, make it glossy, make it slick—

SHELDRAKE

Careful! Those are dirty words! You sound like a bunch of New York critics. Thank you, Miss Schaefer.

BETTY

Goodbye, Mr. Gillis.

GILLIS

Goodbye. Next time I'll write The Naked and the Dead.

Betty leaves.

SHELDRAKE
Well, seems like Zanuck's got himself a baseball picture.

GILLIS
Mr. Sheldrake, I don't want you to think I thought this was going to win any Academy Award.

SHELDRAKE
(His mind free-wheeling) Of course, we're always looking for a Betty Hutton. Do you see it as a Betty Hutton?

GILLIS
Frankly, no.

SHELDRAKE
(Amusing himself) Now wait a minute. If we made it a girls' softball team, put in a few numbers. Might make a cute musical: It Happened in the Bull Pen—the Story of a Woman.

GILLIS
You trying to be funny?—because I'm all out of laughs. I'm up that creek and I need a job.

SHELDRAKE
Sure, Gillis. If something should come along—

GILLIS
Along is no good. I need it now.

SHELDRAKE
Haven't got a thing.

GILLIS
Any kind of assignment. Additional Dialogue.

SHELDRAKE

There's nothing, Gillis. Not even if you were a relative.

GILLIS

(Hating it) Look, Mr. Sheldrake, could you let me have three hundred bucks yourself, as a personal loan?

SHELDRAKE

Could I? Gillis, last year somebody talked me into buying a ranch in the valley. So I borrowed money from the bank so I could pay for the ranch. This year I had to mortgage the ranch so I could keep up my life insurance so I could borrow on the insurance so I could pay my income tax. Now if Dewey had been elected—

GILLIS

Goodbye, Mr. Sheldrake.

DISSOLVE TO:

Ext. Schwab's Drug Store (early afternoon activity)

MOVE IN toward drug store and

DISSOLVE TO:

Int. Schwab's Drug Store

The usual Schwabadero crowd sits at the fountain, gossips at the cigar-stand, loiters by the magazine display. MOVE IN toward the TWO TELEPHONE BOOTHS. In one of them sits Gillis, a stack of nickels in front of him. He's doing a lot of talking into the telephone, hanging up, dropping another nickel, dialing, talking again.

GILLIS' VOICE

After that I drove down to headquarters. That's the way a lot of us think about Schwab's Drug Store. Actors and stock girls and writers. Kind of a combination office, Kaffee-Klatsch and waiting room. Waiting, waiting for the gravy train.

I got myself ten nickels and started sending out a general S.O.S. Couldn't get hold of my agent, naturally. So then I called a pal of mine, name of Artie Green—an awful nice guy, an assistant director. He could let me have twenty, but twenty wouldn't do.

Then I talked to a couple of yes men at Twentieth. To me they said no. Finally I located that agent of

mine. He was hard at work in Bel Air.
Making with the golf sticks.

Gillis hangs up with a curse, opens the door of the booth, emerges, wiping the sweat from his forehead. He walks towards the exit. He is stopped by the voice of

SKOLSKY
Hello, Gillis.

Gillis looks around. At the fountain sits Skolsky, drinking a cup of coffee.

GILLIS
Hello, Mr. Skolsky.

SKOLSKY
Got anything for the column?

GILLIS
Sure. Just sold an original for a hundred grand. The Life of the Warner Brothers. Starring the Ritz Brothers. Playing opposite the Andrew Sisters.

SKOLSKY
(With a sour smile) But don't get me wrong—I love Hollywood.

Gillis walks out.

DISSOLVE TO:

The Bel Air Golf Links

On a sun-dappled green edged with tall sycamores, stands Morino, the agent, a caddy and a nondescript opponent in the background. Gillis has evidently stated his problem already.

MORINO

So you need three hundred dollars? Of course, I could give you three hundred dollars. Only I'm not going to.

GILLIS

No?

MORINO

Gillis, get this through your head. I'm not just your agent. I'm your *friend.*

He sinks his putt and walks toward the next tee, Gillis following him.

GILLIS

How's that about your being my friend?

MORINO

Don't you know the finest things in the world have been written on an empty stomach? Once a talent like yours gets into that Mocambo-Romanoff rut, you're through.

GILLIS

Forget Romanoff's. It's the car I'm talking about. If I lose my car it's like having my legs cut off.

MORINO

Greatest thing that could happen to you. Now you'll *have* to sit behind that typewriter. Now you'll *have* to write.

GILLIS

What do you think I've been doing? I need three hundred dollars.

MORINO

(Icily) Maybe what you need is another agent.

He bends down to tee up his ball. Gillis turns away.

DISSOLVE TO:

Gillis in his open car

Driving down Sunset towards Hollywood. He drives slowly. His mind is working.

GILLIS' VOICE

So I started back towards Hollywood. All the way down Sunset Boulevard I was composing a letter: "To W. W. Agee, Managing Editor, the Dayton Evening Post, Dayton, Ohio. Dear Mr. Halitosis: I am in a terrible predicament. I have just been offered a writer-producer-director contract at seven thousand a week for seven years straight. Shall I do it? Shall I subject myself to the corruption and sham of this tinsel town with its terrible people, or is my place back home where there *are* no people—just plain folks? In other words, how's about that thirty-five-dollar-a-week job behind the rewrite desk?"

Gillis stops his car at a red light by the main entrance to Bel Air. Suddenly his eyes fall on:

Another car

It is a dark-green Dodge business coupe, also waiting for the light to change, but headed in the opposite direction. In it are the two finance company men. They spot Gillis in his car and exchange looks. From across the intersection Gillis recognizes them and pulls down the leather sunshade to screen his face. As the light changes, Gillis gives his car the gun and shoots away. The men narrowly avoid hitting another car as they make a U-turn into oncoming traffic and start after him.

The Chase

Very short, very sharp, told in FLASHES. (Use locations on Sunset between Bel Air and Holmby Hills). The men lose Gillis around a bend, catch sight of him and then—while they are trapped behind a slow-moving truck, he disappears again.

Gillis

He is driving as fast as he dares, keeping an eye out for pursuit in his rear-view mirror. Suddenly his right front tire blows out. Gillis clutches desperately at the steering wheel and manages to turn the careening car into

A driveway

It is overgrown with weeds and screened from the street by bushes and trees. Gillis stops his car about thirty feet from the street and looks back.

The other car

shoots past the driveway, still looking for Gillis.

Gillis	*G I L L I S ' V O I C E*
He gets out of his car to examine the flat tire. Then he looks around to see where he is.	I had landed myself in the driveway of some big mansion that looked run-down and deserted. At the end of the drive was a lovely sight indeed: a great big empty garage, just standing there going to waste . . . If ever there was a place to stash away a limping car with a hot license number . . .
The garage	
It is an enormous, five-car affair, neglected and empty except for a large, dust-covered Isotta-Fraschini propped up on blocks.	
Gillis	There was another occupant in that garage: an enormous foreign-built automobile. The kind that burns up ten gallons to a mile. It had a 1932 license. I figured that's when the owners must have moved out.
He gets back into his car and carefully pilots the limping vehicle into one of the stalls. He closes the garage door and walks up the driveway. In idle curiosity he mounts a stone staircase which leads to the garden, CAMERA IN BACK OF HIM. At the top of the steps he sees the somber pile of	I also figured it was a cinch I couldn't go back to my apartment, so the thing to do was take a bus for Artic Green's and stay there till I promoted that three hundred dollars.

Norma Desmond's house

It is a grandiose, Italianate structure, mottled by the years, gloomy, forsaken, the little formal garden completely gone to seed.

Some people say that when you first see the spot where you're going to die it rings a bell inside you. I didn't hear any bell. It was just big and still, one of those white elephants crazy movie people built in the crazy Twenties.

From somewhere above comes

> *A WOMAN'S VOICE*
> You there!

Gillis turns and looks.

Upstairs loggia

Behind a bamboo blind there is the movement of a dark figure.

> *WOMAN'S VOICE*
> Why are you so late? Why have you kept me waiting so long?

Gillis

He stands flabbergasted. A new noise attracts his attention—the creak of a heavy metal-and-glass door being opened. He turns and sees

The entrance door of the house

Max von Mayerling stands there. He is sixty, and all in black, except for immaculate white cotton gloves, shirt, high, stiff collar and a white bow tie. His coat is shiny black alpaca, his trousers ledger-striped. He is semi-paralyzed. The left side of his mouth is pulled down, and he leans on a rubber-ferruled stick.

> *MAX*
> In here!

Gillis enters the shot.

GILLIS
I just put my car in the garage. I had a blow-out. I thought —

MAX
Go on in.

There is authority in the gesture of his white-gloved hand as he motions Gillis inside.

GILLIS
Look, maybe I'd better take my car —

MAX
Wipe your feet!

Automatically, Gillis wipes his feet on an enormous shabby cocoanut mat.

MAX
You are not dressed properly.

GILLIS
Dressed for what?

THE WOMAN'S VOICE
Max! Have him come up, Max!

MAX
(Gesturing) Up the stairs!

GILLIS
Suppose you listen just for a minute —

MAX
Madame is waiting.

GILLIS
For me? Okay.

Gillis enters.

Int. Norma Desmond's entrance hall

It is grandiose and grim. The whole place is one of those abortions of silent-picture days, with bowling alleys in the cellar and a built-in pipe organ, and beams imported from Italy, with California termites at work on them. Portieres are drawn before all the windows, and only thin slits of sunlight find their way in to fight the few electric bulbs which are always burning.

Gillis starts up the curve of the black marble staircase. It has a wrought-iron rail and a worn velvet rope along the wall.

MAX
(From below) If you need help with the coffin call me.

The oddity of the situation has caught Gillis' imagination. He climbs the stairs with a kind of morbid fascination. At the top he stops, undecided, then turns to the right and is stopped by

WOMAN'S VOICE
This way!

Gillis swings around.

Norma Desmond stands down the corridor next to a doorway from which emerges a flickering light. She is a little woman. There is a curious style, a great sense of high voltage about her. She is dressed in black house pyjamas and black high-heeled pumps. Around her throat there is a leopard-patterned scarf, and wound around her head a turban of the same material. Her skin is very pale, and she is wearing dark glasses.

NORMA

In here. I put him on my massage table in front of the fire. He always liked fires and poking at them with a stick.

Gillis enters the SHOT and she leads him into

Norma Desmond's bedroom

It is a huge, gloomy room hung in white brocade which has become dirty over the years and even slightly torn in a few places. There's a great, unmade gilded bed in the shape of a swan, from which the gold had begun to peel. There is a disorder of clothes and negligees and faded photographs of old-time stars about.

In an imitation baroque fireplace some logs are burning. On the massage table before it lies a small form shrouded under a Spanish shawl. At each end of a baroque pedestal stands a three-branched candelabrum, the candles lighted.

NORMA

I've made up my mind we'll bury him in the garden. Any city laws against that?

GILLIS

I wouldn't know.

NORMA

I don't care anyway. I want the coffin to be white. And I want it specially lined with satin. White, or deep pink.

She picks up the shawl to make up her mind about the color. From under the shawl flops down a dead arm. Gillis stares and recoils a little. It is like a child's arm, only black and hairy.

NORMA

Maybe red, bright flaming red. Gay. Let's make it gay.

Gillis edges closer and glances down. Under the shawl he sees the sad, bearded face of a dead chimpanzee. Norma drops back the shawl.

NORMA
How much will it be? I warn you—don't give me a fancy price just because I'm rich.

GILLIS
Lady, you've got the wrong man.

For the first time, Norma really looks at him through her dark glasses.

GILLIS
I had some trouble with my car. Flat tire. I pulled into your garage till I could get a spare. I thought this was an empty house.

NORMA
It is not. Get out.

GILLIS
I'm sorry, and I'm sorry you lost your friend, and I don't think red is the right color.

NORMA
Get out.

GILLIS
Sure. Wait a minute—haven't I seen you—?

NORMA
Or shall I call my servant?

GILLIS
I know your face. You're Norma Desmond. You used to be in pictures. You used to be big.

NORMA

I *am* big. It's the pictures that got small.

GILLIS

I knew there was something wrong with them.

NORMA

They're dead. They're finished. There was a time when this business had the eyes of the whole wide world. But that wasn't good enough. Oh, no! They wanted the ears of the world, too. So they opened their big mouths, and out came talk, talk, talk . . .

GILLIS

That's where the popcorn business comes in. You buy yourself a bag and plug up your ears.

NORMA

Look at them in the front offices—the master minds! They took the idols and smashed them. The Fairbankses and the Chaplins and the Gilberts and the Valentinos. And who have they got now? Some nobodies—a lot of pale little frogs croaking pish-posh!

GILLIS

Don't get sore at me. I'm not an executive. I'm just a writer.

NORMA

You are! Writing words, words! You've made a rope of words and strangled this business! But there is a microphone right there to catch the last gurgles, and Technicolor to photograph the red, swollen tongue!

GILLIS

Ssh! You'll wake up that monkey.

NORMA

Get out!

Gillis starts down the stairs.

GILLIS

Next time I'll bring my autograph album along, or maybe a hunk of cement and ask for your footprints.

He is halfway down the staircase when he is stopped by

NORMA

Just a minute, you!

GILLIS

Yeah?

NORMA

You're a writer, you said.

GILLIS

Why?

Norma starts down the stairs.

NORMA

Are you or aren't you?

GILLIS

I think that's what it says on my driver's license.

NORMA

And you have written pictures, haven't you?

GILLIS

Sure have. The last one I wrote was about cattle rustlers. Before they were through with it, the whole thing played on a torpedo boat.

Norma has reached him at the bottom of the staircase.

NORMA

I want to ask you something. Come in here.

She leads him into

The huge living room

It is dark and damp and filled with black oak and red velvet furniture which looks like crappy props from the Mark of Zorro set. Along the main wall, a gigantic fireplace has been freezing for years. On the gold piano is a galaxy of photographs of Norma Desmond in her various roles. On one wall is a painting—a California Gold Rush scene, Carthay Circle school. (We will learn later that it hides a motion picture screen.)

One corner is filled with a large pipe organ, and as Norma and Gillis enter, there is a grizzly moaning sound. Gillis looks around.

NORMA

The wind gets in that blasted pipe organ. I ought to have it taken out.

GILLIS

Or teach it a better tune.

Norma has led him to the card tables which stand side by side near a window. They are piled high with papers scrawled in a large, uncertain hand.

NORMA

How long is a movie script these days? I mean, how many pages?

GILLIS

Depends on what it is—a Donald Duck or Joan of Arc.

NORMA

This is to be a very important pictures. I have written it myself. Took me years.

GILLIS

(Looking at the piles of script) Looks like enough for six important pictures.

NORMA

It's the story of Salome. I think I'll have DeMille direct it.

GILLIS

Uh-huh.

NORMA

We've made a lot of pictures together.

GILLIS

And you'll play Salome?

NORMA

Who else?

GILLIS

Only asking. I didn't know you were planning a comeback.

NORMA

I hate that word. It is a return. A return to the millions of people who have never forgiven me for deserting the screen.

GILLIS

Fair enough.

NORMA

Salome—the woman who was all women. You know the story. She was a princess and she was a slave, crawling before John the Baptist, dancing the dance of the Seven Veils. And then she has his head chopped off. He's hers at last. His head is on a golden tray. She kisses his cold, dead lips.

GILLIS
They'll love it in Pomona.

NORMA
(Taking it straight) They will love it every place. (She reaches for a
batch of pages from the heap) Read it. Read the scene just before
she has him killed.

GILLIS
Right now? Never let another writer read your stuff. He may steal
it.

NORMA
I am not afraid. Read it!
(Calling) Max! Max!
   (To Gillis) Sit down. Is there enough light?

GILLIS
I've got twenty-twenty vision.

Max has entered.

NORMA
Bring something to drink.

MAX
Yes, Madame.

He leaves. Norma turns to Gillis again.

NORMA
I said sit down.

There is compulsion in her voice.

Gillis looks at her and starts slowly reading.

Max comes in, wheeling a wicker tea wagon on which are two bottles of champagne and two red Venetian glasses, a box of zwieback and a jar of caviar. Norma sits on her feet, deep in a chair, a gold ring on her forefinger with a clip which holds a cigarette. She gets up and forces on Gillis another batch of script, goes back to her chair.

Shot of the ceiling

PAN DOWN to the moaning organ. PAN OVER TO THE ENTRANCE DOOR. Max opens it, and a solemn-faced man in undertaker's clothes brings in a small white coffin. (Thru these shots the room has been growing duskier).

DISSOLVE TO:

Gillis

reading. The lamp beside him is now really paying its way in the dark room. A lot of the manuscript pages are piled on the floor around his feet. A half-empty champagne glass stands on the arm of his chair.

GILLIS' VOICE

She had a voice like a ringmaster's whip. Somehow I found myself sitting there reading that mad scrawl of hers. Some letters big and arrogant, others as small as fly-specks. I wondered what a handwriting expert would make of it. Max wheeled in some champagne and some caviar. Later, I found out that Max was the only other person in that grim Sunset castle of hers, and I found out a few other things about him. As for her, she sat there curled up like a watch spring. I could sense her eyes on me behind those dark glasses. She kept smoking some Turkish brand of cigarettes. There was a contraption she used to hold them, so her yellow fingers wouldn't get more yellow . . .

GILLIS' VOICE

It sure was a cozy set-up—Max and she and that dead monkey upstairs, and the wind wheezing through that organ once in a while. Later on, just for comedy relief, the real guy arrived, with a baby coffin. It was all done with great dignity. He must have been a very important chimp. The great grandson of King Kong, maybe . . .

It got to be eleven o'clock. I was feeling a little sick at my stomach. It wasn't just that sweet champagne. It was wading through that guck of hers, that mad hodge-pode of melodramatic plots. However, by then I'd started concocting a little plot of my own . . .

THE CAMERA SLOWLY DRAWS BACK to include Norma Desmond sitting in the dusk, just as she was before. Gillis puts down a batch of script. There is a little pause.

NORMA
(Impatiently) Well?

GILLIS
This is fascinating.

NORMA
Of course it is.

GILLIS
Maybe it's a little long and maybe there are some repetitions . . . but you're not a professional writer.

NORMA
I wrote that with my heart.

GILLIS
Sure you did. That's what makes it great. What it needs is a little more dialogue.

NORMA
What for? I can say anything I want with my eyes.

GILLIS
It certainly needs a pair of shears and a blue pencil.

NORMA
I will not have it butchered.

GILLIS
Of course not. But it ought to be organized. Just an editing job. You can find somebody . . .

NORMA
Who? . . .
  (There is a pregnant pause) *You* will do it.

GILLIS
Me? I'm busy. Just finished one script. I'm due on another assignment.

NORMA
I don't care.

GILLIS
You know, I'm pretty expensive. I get five hundred a week.

NORMA
I wouldn't worry about money. I'll make it worth your while.

GILLIS
Maybe I'd better finish reading it.

NORMA
You'll read it tonight.

GILLIS
It's getting kind of late—

NORMA
(Out of nowhere) Are you married, Mr. —?

GILLIS
The name is Gillis. I'm single.

NORMA
Where do you live?

GILLIS
In Hollywood. The Alto Nido Apartments.

NORMA

There's something wrong with your car, you said.

GILLIS

There sure is.

NORMA

(Calling) Max!
  (To Gillis) You're staying here.

GILLIS

I am?

Norma takes off her glasses.

NORMA

Yes, you are. There's a room over the garage. Max!

| THE CAMERA MOVES TOWARD NORMA'S FACE, right up to her eyes. | *GILLIS' VOICE*

She sure could say a lot of things with those pale eyes of hers. They'd been her trade mark. They'd made her the Number One Vamp of another era. I remember a rather florid description in an old fan magazine which said: "Her eyes are like two moonlit waterholes, where strange animals come to drink." |
| DISSOLVE TO:

Small staircase, leading to room over garage

Max, an electric light bulb in his hand, is leading Gillis up. Gillis carries a batch of the manuscipt. | *GILLIS' VOICE*

I took the rest of the script and Max led me to the room over the garage. I thought I'd wangled myself a pretty good deal. I'd do a little work, my car would be safe down below, until I got some money out of her . . . |

Max pushes open a door at the top of the stairs.

> MAX
> (Opening the door) I made your bed this afternoon.

> GILLIS
> Thanks.
>   (On second thought) How did you know I was going to stay, *this afternoon*?

Max doesn't answer. He walks across to the bed, screws a bulb in the open socket above it. The light goes on, revealing:

A gabled bedroom

There are dirty windows on two sides, and dingy wallpaper on the cracked plaster walls. For furniture there is a neatly made bed, a table and a few chairs which might have been discarded from the main house.

> MAX
> This room has not been used for a long time.

> GILLIS
> It will never make House Beautiful. I guess it's O.K. for one night.

Max gives him an enigmatic look.

> MAX
> (Pointing) There is the bathroom. I put in soap and a toothbrush.

> GILLIS
> Thanks.
>   (He starts taking off his coat) Say, she's quite a character, that Norma Desmond.

MAX

She was the greatest. You wouldn't know. You are too young. In one week she got seventeen thousand fan letters. Men would bribe her manicurist to get clippings from her fingernails. There was a Maharajah who came all the way from Hyderabad to get one of her stockings. Later, he strangled himself with it.

GILLIS

I sure turned into an interesting driveway.

MAX

You did, sir.

He goes out. Gillis looks after him, hangs his coat over a chair, walks over to the window, pulls down the rickety Venetian blind. As he does so, he looks down at:

GILLIS' VOICE

I figured he was a little crazy. Maybe he'd had a stroke—part of his brain wasn't hitting on all cylinders. Come to think of it, the whole place was like that—half paralyzed, crumbling apart in slow motion.

The tennis court of the Desmond house (moonlight)

The cement surface is cracked in many places, and weeds are growing high.

GILLIS' VOICE

There was a tennis court, or rather the ghost of a tennis court, with faded markings and a sagging net.

Gillis—in the window

He looks away from the court to;

The Desmond swimming pool

There is no water in it, and hunks of mosaic which lines its enormous basin are broken away.

And of course she had a pool. Who didn't then? Mabel Normand and John Gilbert must have swum in it ten thousand midnights ago, and Vilma Banky and Rod LaRoque. It was empty now, except for some rubbish and something stirring down there . . .

Gillis—In the window

He stares down, his stomach slowly turning.

The swimming pool

At the bottom of the basin a great rat is eating a decaying orange. From the inlet pipe crawl two other rats, who join battle with the first rat over the orange.

Gillis—In the window

He starts away, but something attracts his attention. He turns back and looks down again.

GILLIS' VOICE

I thought I caught the flicker of a light. There was something else going on below—the last rites for that hairy old chimp. She was always playing some sort of part. This time she was Lady Macbeth on a tragic Scottish moor, or a bereaved empress queen mourning her dead prince imperial . . .

The lawn below

Norma Desmond and Max are carrying the white coffin towards a small grave which has been dug in the dead turf. Norma carries one of the candelabra, all of its candles flickering in the wind. They reach the grave and lower the coffin into it. Then, Norma lighting his task with the candelabrum, Max takes a spade from the loose earth and starts filling in the grave.

Gillis—In the window

He watches the scene below, then turns into the room, goes to the door to lock it. There is no key, and only a hole where the lock has been gouged out. Gillis moves a heavy overstuffed chair in front of the door, then walks towards the bed, throws himself on it, picking up some of the manuscript pages to read.

GILLIS' VOICE

It was all very queer, but queerer things were yet to come . . . !

DISSOLVE:

1949

MARTIN AMIS

Money

CALIFORNIA, LAND of my dreams and my longing.

You've seen me in New York and you know what I'm like there but in LA, man, I tell you, I'm more of a high-achiever – all fizz and push, a fixer, a bustler, a real new-dealer. Last December for a whole week my thirty-minute short *Dean Street* was being shown daily at the Pantheon of Celestial Arts. In squeaky-clean restaurants, round smoggy poolsides, in jungly jacuzzis I made my deals. Business went well and it all looked possible. It was in the pleasure area, as usual, that I found I had a problem.

In LA, you can't do anything unless you drive. Now *I* can't do anything unless I drink. And the drink–drive combination, it really isn't possible out there. If you so much as loosen your seatbelt or drop your ash or pick your nose, then it's Alcatraz autopsy with the questions asked later. Any indiscipline, you feel, any variation, and there's a bullhorn, a set of scope sights, and a coptered pig drawing a bead on your rug.

So what can a poor boy do? You come out of the hotel, the Vraimont. Over boiling Watts the downtown skyline carries a smear of God's green snot. You walk left, you walk right, you are a bank rat on a busy river. This restaurant serves no drink, this one serves no meat, this one serves no heterosexuals. You can get your chimp shampooed, you can get your dick tattooed, twenty-four hour, but can you get lunch? And should you see a sign on the far side of the street flashing BEEF-BOOZE – NO STRINGS, then you can forget it. The only way to get across the road is to be born there. All the ped-xing signs say DON'T WALK, all of them, all the time. That is the message, the content of Los Angeles: don't walk. Stay inside. Don't walk. Drive. Don't walk. Run! I tried the cabs. No use. The cabbies are all

Saturnians who aren't even sure whether this is a right planet or a left planet. The first thing you have to do, every trip, is teach them to drive.

I got drunk and dialled Hire-A-Heap and rented a scarred Boomerang on a budget four-day buy. I bombed around with a pint between my thighs. Bel-Air, Malibu, Venice. Then on the last night I made my big mistake, and hit that bad business I told you about. I don't like to sound judgmental, but it really was a big mistake. I was surging down Sunset Boulevard: purely on impulse I hung a left near Scheldt's, where I've seen these sweet little black chicks parading in tiny pastel running-shorts . . . Anyhow the upshot is, one way or another I'm lying in the front seat of the Boomerang with my trousers round my knees and copping a twenty-dollar blowjob from a speed-fueled Zulu called Agnes. I mean it's incredibly reasonable, don't you think? What a fine country. What value. With sterling in the shape it's in, that's barely nine quid! But Agnes and I have a problem. 'This is why they're called hard-ons,' I remember explaining to her. 'They're not at all easy. They're very difficult.' Agnes is losing patience and revenue, I've practically got my legs sticking out of the Boomerang window, when there's this heavy handslap on the roof of the car.

I thought: law. The sex police! I straightened my neck. A glamorous, dressing-gowned housewife was staring through the open side window, her face framed by my shoes. 'Hurry it up, pal,' she said. 'You're in my drive.' Instantly, as if it were a bad oyster, Agnes spat my dick out of her mouth and started shrieking back at this loathed adversary of hers—Agnes's language, it was unimaginable: even I was grossed out by it. She swore detailed vengeance on the woman, her dogs, her kids, with intimate reference to various feminine rudiments and effluvia that I for one had never come across. 'Okay it's the cops,' said the lady finally, and strode back towards the house . . . I was thrashing and clawing but with Agnes still slumped on my middle and the whisky bottle and everything I couldn't seem to writhe my way upright. Then the door behind my head jerked open, the car light came on like a flashbulb, and there was a seven-foot black pimp snarling down at me with a mahogany baseball bat in his fist.

Well, you don't ever feel more naked than that. No—you never do. Something about the bat itself, the resined or saddlesoaped grain of its surface, offered unwelcome clarity, reminding me why I had stayed away from Scheldt's and the sweet black chicks and their bargain blowjobs. *This is all very serious and violent and criminal and mean. You cannot go slumming, not here, because slums bite back.* As Agnes wriggled out of the far door the big pimp raised his hammer. I clenched my eyes. No quarter. I heard a grunt, a hum of air, a bloodstunning crack, then with oddly exact and flowing movements I sat up saying *'Money',* took my wallet from its holster, fanned five twenties at the sweating black face, wedged shut the door, made the triple-ring sign, and drove sedately out of Rosalind Court. Next, the machine squeal of sirens on my tail. Leaving a continuous, scalding double-tyretrack in my wake, I rocketed on to Sunset Boulevard, jumped three lights and made a spectacular crash-landing in the lot beneath the Vraimont. I slid out the door and made a dash for the lift. I got to my feet, pulled up the trousers which shackled my ankles, and tried again. Lucky lucky lucky, oh lucky, I kept saying, as I washed the blood off my nose in Room 666. They didn't even notice the smashed front lights and the vicious new welt on the Boomerang doorframe when I slinked back to Hire-A-Heap the following day. I leaned over in my boxy suit and re-signed the credit slip, my bitten fingers shimmering over the scorched trunk. Behind my back, under showboat lights, Sunset Boulevard sailed on down its slope.

An hour later I was fastening my safety-belt at LAX. First class: the Pantheon of Celestial Arts—their treat. Toasting John Self with premixed martinis, I too was a cocktail shaker of hilarity and awe. I had just been reading in the *Daily Minute* about the string of beatings and manslaughters in Rosalind Court: the night before last a Jap computer expert and a German dentist had been found in a parking lot with their faces stomped off. I think I was in shock, or undergoing reaction. 'You're so lucky, you're so *lucky*,' I murmured, staring down at the rocky Rockies or the Smokies or the Ropies through cloud-cover made of snow and contour tracing . . . In the next throne along lounged an elegant young man—summer business suit, Cal tan, thick, unlayered rug: I took him for an actor. He glanced up from his hardback and sipped his champagne. He raised the glass. 'Here's to luck,' he said. 'And to money.' Well, I didn't need much prompting and soon babbled out all my dreams and dreads. It transpired that he had been scouting at the Festival. He'd seen *Dean Street*, and liked what he saw. And to follow? I told him about *Bad Money*—another short, no big deal. We talked, we made plans, we exchanged numbers, as you do on aeroplanes: it's the booze, it's the canned air and the rich-quick stories, it's the pornography of travel.

1984

HENRY MILLER

Soirée in Hollywood

MY FIRST evening in Hollywood. It was so typical that I almost thought it had been arranged for me. It was by sheer chance, however, that I found myself rolling up to the home of a millionaire in a handsome black Packard. I had been invited to dinner by a perfect stranger. I didn't even know my host's name. Nor do I know it now.

The first thing which struck me, on being introduced all around, was that I was in the presence of wealthy people, people who were bored to death and who were all, including the octogenarians, already three sheets to the wind. The host and hostess seemed to take pleasure in acting as bartenders. It was hard to follow the conversation because everybody was talking at cross purposes. The important thing was to get an edge on before sitting down to the table. One old geezer who had recently recovered from a horrible automobile accident was having his fifth old-fashioned—he was proud of the fact, proud that he could swill it like a youngster even though he was partially crippled. Every one thought he was a marvel.

There wasn't an attractive woman about, except the one who had brought me to the place. The men looked like business men, except for one or two who looked like aged strike-breakers. There was one fairly young couple, in their thirties, I should say. The husband was a typical go-getter, one of those ex-football players who go in for publicity or insurance or the stock market, some clean all-American pursuit in which you run no risk of soiling your hands. He was a graduate of some Eastern University and had the intelligence of a high-grade chimpanzee.

That was the set-up. When every one had been properly soused dinner was announced. We seated ourselves at a long table, elegantly decorated, with three or four glasses beside each plate. The ice was abundant, of course. The service began, a dozen flunkeys buzzing at your elbow like horse flies. There was a surfeit of everything; a poor man would have had sufficient with the hors-d'oeuvre alone. As they ate, they became more discursive, more argumentative. An elderly thug in a tuxedo who had the complexion of a boiled lobster was railing against labor agitators. He had a religious strain, much to my amazement, but it was more like Torquemada's than Christ's. President Roosevelt's name almost gave him an apoplectic fit. Roosevelt, Bridges, Stalin, Hitler—they were all in the same class to him. That is to say, they were anathema. He had an extraordinary appetite which served, it seemed, to stimulate his adrenal glands. By the time he had reached the meat course he was talking about hanging being too good for some people. The hostess, meanwhile, who was seated at his elbow, was carrying on one of those delightful inconsequential conversations with the person opposite her. She had left some beautiful dachshunds in Biarritz, or was it Sierra Leone, and to believe her, she was greatly worried about them. In times like these, she was saying, people forget about animals. People can be so cruel, especially in time of war. Why, in Peking the servants had run away and left her with forty trunks to pack—it was outrageous. It was so good to be back in California. God's own country, she called it. She hoped the war wouldn't spread to America. Dear me, where was one to go now? You couldn't feel safe anywhere, except in the desert perhaps.

The ex-football player was talking to some one at the far end of the table in a loud voice. It happened to be an Englishwoman and he was insulting her roundly and openly for daring to arouse sympathy for the English in this country. "Why don't you go back to England?" he shouted at the top of his voice. "What are you doing here? You're a menace. We're not fighting to hold the British Empire together. You're a menace. You ought to be expelled from the country."

The woman was trying to say that she was not English but Canadian, but she couldn't make herself heard above the din. The octogenarian, who was now sampling the champagne, was talking about the automobile accident. Nobody was paying any attention to him. Automobile accidents were too common—every one at the table had been in a smash-up at one time or another. One doesn't make a point about such things unless one is feeble-minded.

The hostess was clapping her hands frantically—she wanted to tell us a little story about an experience she had had in Africa once, on one of her safaris.

"Oh, can that!" shouted the football player. "I want to find out why this great country of ours, in the most crucial moment . . . "

"Shut up!" screamed the hostess. "You're drunk."

"That makes no difference," came his booming voice. "I want to know if we're all hundred percent Americans—and if not why not. I suspect that we have some traitors in our midst," and because I hadn't been taking part in any of the conversation he gave me a fixed, drunken look which was intended to make me declare myself. All I could do was smile. That seemed to infuriate him. His eyes roved about the table challengingly and finally, sensing an antagonist worthy of his mettle, rested on the aged, Florida-baked strike-breaker. The latter was at that moment quietly talking to the person beside him about his good friend, Cardinal So-and-so. He, the Cardinal, was always very good to the poor, I heard him say. A very gentle hard-working man, but he would tolerate no nonsense from the dirty labor agitators who were stirring up revolution, fomenting class hatred, preaching anarchy. The more he talked about his holy eminence, the Cardinal, the more he foamed at the mouth. But his rage in no way affected his appetite. He was carnivorous, bibulous, querulous, cantankerous and poisonous as a snake. One could almost see the bile spreading through his varicose veins. He was a man who had spent millions of dollars of the public's money to help the needy, as he put it. What he meant was to prevent the poor from organizing and fighting for their rights. Had he not been dressed like a banker he would have passed for a hod carrier. When he grew angry he not only became flushed but his whole body quivered like guava. He became so intoxicated by his own venom that finally he overstepped the bounds and began denouncing President Roosevelt as a crook and a traitor, among other things. One of the guests, a woman, protested. That brought the football hero to his feet. He said that no man could insult the President of the United States in his presence. The whole table was soon in an uproar. The flunkey at my elbow had just filled the huge liquor glass with some marvelous cognac. I took a sip and sat back with a grin, wondering how it would all end. The louder the altercation the more peaceful I became. *"How do you like your new boarding house, Mr. Smith?"* I heard President McKinley saying to his secretary. Every night Mr. Smith, the president's private secretary, used to visit Mr. McKinley at his home and read aloud to him the amusing letters which he had selected from the daily correspondence. The president, who was overburdened with affairs of state, used to listen silently from his big armchair by the fire: it was his sole recreation. At the end he would always ask *"How do you like your new boarding house, Mr. Smith?"* So worn out by his duties he was that he couldn't think of anything else to say at the close of these séances. Even after Mr. Smith had left his boarding house and taken a room at a hotel President McKinley continued to say *"How do you like your new boarding house, Mr. Smith?"* Then came the Exposition and Csolgosz, who had no idea what a simpleton the president was, assassinated him. There was something wretched and incongruous about murdering a man like McKinley. I remember the incident only because that same day the horse that my aunt was using for a buggy ride got the blind staggers and ran into a lamp post and when I was going to the hospital to see my aunt the extras were out already and young as I was I understood that a great tragedy had befallen the nation. At the same time I felt sorry for Csolgosz—that's the strange thing about the incident. I don't know why I felt sorry for him, except that in some vague way I realized that the punishment meted out to him would be greater than the crime merited. Even at that tender age I felt that punishment was criminal. I couldn't understand why people should be punished—I don't yet. I couldn't even understand why God had the right to punish us for our sins. And of course, as I later realized, God doesn't punish us—we punish ourselves.

Thoughts like these were floating through my head when suddenly I became aware that people were leaving the table. The meal wasn't over yet, but the guests were departing. Something had happened while I was reminiscing. Pre-civil war days, I thought to myself. Infantilism rampant again. And if Roosevelt is assassinated they will make another Lincoln of him. Only this time the slaves will still be slaves. Meanwhile I overhear some one saying what a wonderful president Melvyn Douglas would make. I prick up my ears. I wonder do they mean Melvyn Douglas, the movie star? Yes, that's who they mean. He has a great mind, the woman is saying. And character. And *savoir faire*. Thinks I to myself "and who will the vice-president be, may I ask? Shure and it's not Jimmy Cagney you're thinkin' of?" But the woman is not worried about the vice-presidency. She had been to a palmist the other day and learned some interesting things about herself. Her life line was broken. "Think of it," she said, "all these years and I never knew it was broken. What do you suppose is going to happen? Does it mean war? Or do you think it means an accident?"

The hostess was running about like a wet hen. Trying to rustle up enough hands for a game of bridge. A desperate soul, surrounded by the booty of a thousand battles. "I understand you're a writer," she said, as she tried to carom from my corner of the room to the bar. "Won't you have something to drink—a highball or something? Dear me, I don't know what's come over everybody this evening. I do hate to hear these political discussions. That young man is positively rude. Of course I don't approve of insulting the President of the United States in public but just the same he might have used a little more tact. After all, Mr. So-and-so is an elderly man. He's entitled to some respect, don't you think? Oh, there's So-and-so!" and she dashed off to greet a cinema star who had just dropped in.

The old geezer who was still tottering about handed me a highball. I tried to tell him that I didn't want any but he insisted that I take it anyway. He wanted to have a word with me, he said, winking at me as though he had something very confidential to impart.

"My name is Harrison," he said. "H-a-r-r-i-s-o-n," spelling it out as if it were a difficult name to remember.

"Now what is your name, may I ask?"

"My name is Miller—"M-i-l-l-e-r," I answered, spelling it out in Morse for him.

"Miller! Why, that's a very easy name to remember. We had a druggist on our block by that name. Of course. *Miller*. Yes, a very common name."

"So it is," I said.

"And what are you doing out her, Mr. Miller? You're a stranger, I take it?"

"Yes," I said, "I'm just a visitor."

"You're in business, are you?"

"No, hardly. I'm just visiting California."

"I see. Well, where do you come from—the Middle West?"

"No, from New York."

"From New York City? Or from up State?"

"From the city."

"And have you been here very long?"

"No, just a few hours."

"A few hours? My, my . . . well, that's interesting. Very interesting. And will you be staying long, Mr. Miller?"

"I don't know. It depends."

"I see. Depends on how you like it here, is that it?"

"Yes, exactly."

"Well, it's a grand part of the world, I can tell you that. No place like California, I always say. Of course I'm not a native. But I've been out here almost thirty years now. Wonderful climate. And wonderful people, too."

"I suppose so," I said, just to string him along. I was curious to see how long the idiot would keep up his infernal nonsense.

"You're in business you say?"

"No, I'm not."

"On a vacation, is that it?"

"No, not precisely. I'm an ornithologist, you see."

"A what? Well, that's interesting."

"Very," I said, with great solemnity.

"Then you may be staying with us for a while, is that it?"

"That's hard to say. I may stay a week and I may stay a year. It all depends. Depends on what specimens I find."

"I see. Interesting work, no doubt."

"Very!"

"Have you ever been to California before, Mr. Miller?"

"Yes, twenty-five years ago."

"Well, well, is that so? *Twenty-five years ago!* And now you're back again."

"Yes, back again."

"Were you doing the same thing when you were here before?"

"You mean ornithology?"

"Yes, that's it."

"No, I was digging ditches then."

"Digging ditches? You mean you were—*digging ditches*?"

"Yes, that's it, Mr. Harrison. It was either dig ditches or starve to death."

" Well, I'm glad you don't have to dig ditches any more. It's not much fun—*digging ditches*, is it?"

"No, especially if the ground is hard. Or if your back is weak. Or vice versa. Or let's say your mother has just been put in the mad house and the alarm goes off too soon."

"I beg your pardon! *What did you say?*"

"If things are not just right, I said. You know what I mean—bunnions, lumbago, scrofula. It's different now, of course. I have my birds and other pets. Mornings I used to watch the sun rise. Then I would saddle the jackass—I had two and the other fellow had three. . . . "

"This was in California, Mr. Miller?"

"Yes, twenty-five years ago. I had just done a stretch in San Quentin. . . . "

"San Quentin?"

"Yes, attempted suicide. I was really gaga but that didn't make any difference to them. You see, when my father set the house afire one of the horses kicked me in the temple. I used to get fainting fits and then after a time I got homicidal spells and finally I became suicidal. Of course I didn't know that the revolver was loaded. I took a pot shot at my sister, just for fun, and luckily I missed her. I tried to explain it to the judge but he wouldn't listen to me. I never carry a revolver any more. If I have to defend myself I use a jack-knife. The best thing, of course, is to use your knee. . . . "

"Excuse me, Mr. Miller, I have to speak to Mrs. So-and-so a moment. Very interesting what you say. *Very interesting indeed.* We must talk some more. Excuse me just a moment. . . . "

I slipped out of the house unnoticed and started to walk towards the foot of the hill. The highballs, the red and the white wines, the champagne, the cognac were gurgling inside me like a sewer. I had no idea where I was, whose house I had been in or whom I had been introduced to. Perhaps the boiled thug was an ex-Governor of the

State. Perhaps the hostess was an ex-movie star, a light that had gone out forever. I remembered that some one had whispered in my ear that So-and-so had made a fortune in the opium traffic in China. Lord Haw-Haw probably. The Englishwoman with the horse face may have been a prominent novelist—or just a charity worker. I thought of my friend Fred, now Private Alfred Perlès, No. 13802023 in the 137th Pioneer Corps or something like that. Fred would have sung the Lorelei at the dinner table or asked for a better brand of cognac or made grimaces at the hostess. Or he might have gone to the telephone and called up Gloria Swanson, pretending to be Aldous Huxley or Chatto & Windus of Wimbledon. Fred would never have permitted the dinner to become a fiasco. Everything else failing he would have slipped his silky paw in some one's bosom, saying as he always did— "The left one is better. Fish it out, won't you please?"

I think frequently of Fred in moving about the country. He was always so damned eager to see America. His picture of America was something like Kafka's. It would be a pity to disillusion him. And yet who can say? He might enjoy it hugely. He might not see anything but what he chose to see. I remember my visit to his own Vienna. Certainly it was not the Vienna I had dreamed of. And yet today, when I think of Vienna, I see the Vienna of my dreams and not the one with bed bugs and broken zithers and stinking drains.

I wobble down the canyon road. It's very California somehow. I like the scrubby hills, the weeping trees, the desert coolness. I had expected more fragrance in the air.

The stars are out in full strength. Turning a bend in the road I catch a glimpse of the city below. The illumination is more faërique than in other American cities. The red seems to predominate. A few hours ago, towards dusk, I had a glimpse of it from the bedroom window of the woman on the hill. Looking at it through the mirror on her dressing table it seemed even more magical. It was like looking into the future from the narrow window of an oubliette. Imagine the Marquis de Sade looking at the city of Paris through the bars of his cell in the Bastille. Los Angeles gives one the feeling of the future more strongly than any city I know of. A bad future, too, like something out of Fritz Lang's feeble imagination. *Good-bye, Mr. Chips!*

Walking along one of the Neon-lit streets. A shop window with

Nylon stockings. Nothing in the window but a glass leg filled with water and a sea horse rising and falling like a feather sailing through heavy air. Thus we see how Surrealism penetrates to every nook and corner of the world. Dali meanwhile is in Bowling Green, Va., thinking up a loaf of bread 30 feet high by 125 feet long, to be removed from the oven stealthily while every one sleeps and placed circumspectly in the main square of a big city, say Chicago or San Francisco. Just a loaf of bread, enormous of course. No raison d'être. No propaganda. And tomorrow night two loaves of bread, placed simultaneously in two big cities, say New York and New Orleans. Nobody knows who brought them or why they are there. And the next night three loaves of bread—one in Berlin or Bucharest this time. And so on, ad infinitum. Tremendous, no? Would push the war news off the front page. That's what Dali thinks, at any rate. Very interesting. *Very interesting, indeed.* Excuse me now, I have to talk to a lady over in the corner. . . .

Tomorrow I will discover Sunset Boulevard. Eurythmic dancing, ball room dancing, tap dancing, artistic photography, ordinary photography, lousy photography, electro-fever treatment, internal douche treatment, ulta-violet ray treatment, elocution lessons, psychic readings, institutes of religion, astrological demonstrations, hands read, feet manicured, elbows massaged, faces lifted, warts removed, fat reduced, insteps raised, corsets fitted, busts vibrated, corns removed, hair dyed, glasses fitted, soda jerked, hangovers cured, headaches driven away, flatulence dissipated, business improved, limousines rented, the future made clear, the war made comprehensible, octane made higher and butane lower, drive in and get indigestion, flush the kidneys, get a cheap car wash, stay awake pills and go to sleep pills, Chinese herbs are very good for you and without a Coca-cola life is unthinkable. From the car window it's like a strip teaser doing the St. Vitus dance—a corny one.

1945

SARAH BIXBY SMITH

Adobe Days

Los ANGELES was about ninety years old and I about one when we first met, neither of us, I am afraid, taking much notice of the other. For over twenty years San Francisco had been a city, a most interesting and alive city, making so much stir in the world that people forgot that Los Angeles was the older; that her birth had been ordained by the governor and attended with formal rites of the church and salutes from the military way back in 1781, when the famous revolution on the east coast was just drawing to a successful close. Until the stirring days of '49, San Francisco was insignificance on sand hills. Then her rise was sudden and glorious and the Queen of the Angels was humble. But she was angelic only in name. She was a typical frontier town with primitive, flat-roofed dwellings of sun-dried bricks, much like those built in ancient Assyria or Palestine. Saloons and gambling houses were out of proportion in number, and there were murders every day. The present crime wave is nothing in comparison.

My father first saw Los Angeles in January, 1854, when he was camped with his sheep on the Rancho San Pasqual; his arrival was a few months later than that of Mr. Harris Newmark, who, in his book *Sixty Years in Southern California,* so vividly describes the village as he found it.

By the time I knew it there had been a great change. There were some sidewalks, water was piped to the houses, gas had been introduced; several public school buildings had been built; there were three newspapers, *The Star, The Express,* and *The Herald.* The public library had been founded,—it occupied rooms in the Downey Block where the Federal Building now stands, and Mary Foy, one of Los Angeles's distinguished women, had begun her public service as a young girl in attendance. Compared with what it had been twenty years before, Los Angeles was a modern, civilized city; compared with what it is now, it was a little frontier town. At school I once learned its population to be 11,311.

We lived first on Temple Street, near Charity. Once Los Angeles boasted Faith and Hope Streets as well, but only Hope remains, for Faith has turned to Flower, and Charity masquerades as Grand.

Next door to us lived a Jewish family whose girls sat on the front porch and amazed me by crocheting on Sunday. I had not known that any Jews existed outside the Bible. Perhaps this family was the nucleus for the present large colony of Hebrews that now fills the neighborhood.

Temple Street was new and open for only a few blocks. Bunker Hill Avenue was the end of the settlement, a row of scattered houses along the ridge fringing the sky. Beyond that we looked over empty, grassy hills to the mountains. Going down the first hillside and over towards Beaudry's reservoir for a picnic, I once found maidenhair ferns under some brush, and was frightened by what sounded like a rattlesnake—probably only a cicada. Court Street disappeared in a hollow at Hope, where a pond was made interesting by a large flock of white ducks.

Across the street from us on top of a hill that is now gone, at the head of a long flight of wide steps, stood "The Horticultural Pavilion," destroyed a few years later by fire. It was replaced by Hazard's Pavilion, an equally barn-like, wooden building on the site of the present Philharmonic Auditorium. The first Pavilion held county fairs, conventions, and operas. It was in this place that I once had a great disappointment, for when I was hearing *Pinafore* a child ahead of me suddenly coughed and whooped, and I was removed with haste just at the most entrancing moment. The opera had been put on in London first in the spring of '78. It had reached Los Angeles by '79, and we revelled in its wit and melody with the rest of the world.

It must have been somewhat later than this that the city took such pride in the singing of one of its own girls, Mamie Perry (Mrs. Modini-Wood) who was educated abroad and made her debut in Italy. Another name that will recall many a concert and social event to old timers is that of Madame Mara.

In this building I once saw a strange instrument, a box into which one could speak and be heard half a mile away at a similar contraption—a very meek and lowly promise of our present telephone system.

At this fair, where there were exhibited fruits, jellies and cakes, quilts and long strings of buttons, when the mania for collecting them was at its height, I remember that some ladies, interested in the new Orphans' Home, served New England dinners, in a room decked as an old fashioned kitchen with spinning wheels and strings of corn and drying apples. Among them were my mother and Mrs. Dan Stevens, two slender, dark-haired young women, wearing colonial costume and high combs—my mother, who so soon after left this world, and Mrs. Stevens, still among us, loved and honored for her many good works.

Mrs. Stevens tells me that this was at the time of the visit of President and Mrs. Hayes and a party of government officials, the first president of the United States to come to California. All Los Angeles turned out to welcome them, although there was enough bitter partisan feeling left to cause some neighbors of ours to walk past him in line while refusing to shake the hand of the man who they believed usurped Tilden's rightful place.

The celebration began with speaking from a grandstand built in front of the Baker Block, followed by a reception given to Mrs. Hayes and the ladies of the party in the parlors of the fashionable St. Elmo Hotel, still standing but now fallen to low estate.

After this the presidential party went to the county fair at the pavilion where there was more speaking, a public reception and a formal dinner. Dr. David Barrows contributes as his memory of this great occasion—the memory of a small boy who had been brought down from the Ojai Valley—his amazement to observe that Secretary Sherman kept his cigar in his mouth while making his address. It was during this speech that a little boy came forward bringing a great bouquet, the gift of the local florist, but suffered so from stage fright that he refused to mount the platform and my small sister, standing near, was substituted. She marched serenely across the stage, delivered the flowers to Mrs. Hayes, was kissed by her, then by the speaker, and final glory, by the President himself. I am sure it was the most lime-lighty moment of Nan's modest life.

This bouquet was not the only gift we afforded our distinguished visitor. The other was a cup and saucer, fearfully and wonderfully made of sectors of red, white and blue cambric, stitched round and round until it was stiff by a little hole-in-the-wall sewing-machine agent.

After inspecting our fruits, vegetables, cookery, button strings and other fancy work the party was entertained at dinner by the leading women of Los Angeles in the improvised New England kitchen at the fair. The city council granted them the privilege and appropriated toward expense the generous sum of twenty-five dollars, all the council could afford toward banqueting the most distinguished party that had yet visited the City of the Queen of the Angels, so said Mayor Toberman. But every grower of fine turkeys or prize fruit or vegetables and every notable maker of preserves brought in offerings in kind so that in spite of the council's thrift a most generous feast was spread before our guests.

Speaking of politics recalls the wonderful torch-light processions of a later period when I, with my cousins, shouting little Republicans, perched on the fence at their residence on the corner of Second and Broadway and delightedly recognized our fathers under the swinging, smoky lights.

I happened to be in Maine during the Blaine-Cleveland campaign and once rode upon a train to which Mr. Blaine's special car was attached. It interested me to see that when he got out at one station for a hasty cup of coffee at a lunch counter, he poured the hot liquid into his saucer to drink. Was that doing politics, being one of the people, or was it simply that the mouth of a presidential candidate is as susceptible to heat as that of an ordinary mortal? I was much edified, as I was not accustomed to saucer-drinking. When the train reached Boston towards midnight, it was met by a most gorgeous torchlight parade and a blare of music.

When Garfield died, Los Angeles had a memorial service and a long daylight procession headed by a "Catafalque," (a large float, gruesomely black), on which one of my schoolmates, Laura Chauvin, rode to represent, I suppose, a mourning angel. Later its black broadcloth draperies were used to make souvenirs and sold for some deserving cause. We purchased a pin-ball the size of a dollar, decorated with a green and white embroidered thistle,—a curious memento of a murdered president.

But I have been lured by memories of processions as is a small boy by martial music, away from my ordered account of where I have lived in Los Angeles. The second year we moved to the Shepherd house, (so-called because of its owner), where presently my brother, Llewellyn Bixby, junior, in direct answer to my prayers, came through the ceiling of the front bedroom straight into the apron of Mrs. Maitland,—a two-day-late birthday present for me. So I was told. My sceptical faculty was dormant.

This house still stands at the top of the precipice made by the cutting of first Street between Hill and Olive Streets.

The lot in front was very steep, with zig-zag paths and terraces, in one of which was a grove of banana trees, where fruit formed, but, owing to insufficient heat, never ripened well. Do you know the cool freshness of the furled, new, pale green leaves? Or how delightful it is to help the wind shred the old ones into fringe? One by one the red and gray covers for the circled blossoms drop, and make fetching little leather caps for playing children.

In those days the hill had not been hacked away to make streets, and where now is a great gash to let First Street through there was then a breezy, open hill-top, whereon grew brush and wild-flowers. The poppies in those days were eschscholtzias (the learning to spell the name was a feat of my eighth year), and were not subjected to the ignominy of being painted with poinsettias on fringed leather souvenirs for tourists. The yellow violets were gallitas, little roosters, perhaps because in the hands of children they fought to the death, their necks hooked together until one or the other was decapitated. The brodiaeas, or wild hyacinths, sometimes now called "rubber-necks," were called cacomites, (four syllables), a word of Aztec origin brought to California by people from Mexico where it was applied to a different flower but one having like this one a sweet edible root.

Between the weeds and bushes there were bare spots of ground where, by careful searching, one might find faint circles about the size of a "two-bit" piece. Wise ones knew that these marked the trap doors of tarantula nests. It was sport to try to pry one open, with mother spider holding it closed. We young vandals would dig out the nests, interested for a moment in the silky lining and the tiny babies and then would throw away the wrecked home of the gorgeous black velvet creatures that did no harm on the open hill side.

At this house Harry and I conducted an extensive "essence factory," collecting old bottles far and near, and filling them with vari-colored liquids, obtained by soaking or steeping different flowers and leaves. We used to drink the brew made from eucalyptus leaves. The pepper infusion was pale, like tea; that made from old geraniums was of a horrible odor,—hence we liked to inveigle innocent grown folks into smelling it. The cactus solution was thick, like castor oil, and we considered it our most valuable product, having arrived thus early at the notion that difficulty of preparation adds to the cost of a manufactured article.

North of us were several houses containing children—and here I found my first girl play-mates—Grace and Susie, Bertha and Eileen. The level street at Court and Hill, protected on three sides by grades too steep for horses, was our safe neighborhood playground. I never go through the tunnel that now has pierced the hill without hearing, above the roar of the Hollywood car, the patter of flying feet, the rhythms of the witch dances, the thud-thud of hop-scotch, the shouting boys and girls defending goals in Prisoner's Base, the old, old song of London Bridge, or the "Intry mintry cutry corn" that determined who was "it" for the twilight game of Hide-and-Seek—and then the varied toned bells in the hands of mothers who called the children home.

We played school, jacks, marbles, tag, and an adaption of Peck's Bad Boy, and, between whiles, dolls. Even Harry played with them when we were still youngsters—say eight or nine. He didn't seem young to me then—he was just himself. I called him "Hab." My aunt tells of finding us once about our housekeeping, he doing the doll family washing, and I papering the house. In our menage there was no sex distinction as to the work to be done.

We girls, as we grew a little older, had a collection of small dolls, none over four inches long, and the various marriages, deaths, and parties kept us busy. I tailored for the whole group, having apparently a talent for trousers, which early experience undoubtedly encouraged me in later life to gather in all the stray pantaloons to cut over into knickerbockers for my numerous boys.

Raids on the Chinese vegetable wagon provided supplies for our cooking over a row of small, outdoor fire-places we had built in a low bank in our yard. Once my mother was much disturbed to find a little pot of squirrel meat cooking on the stove. She needn't have worried, for I knew as well as she that strychnine, slipped into a small piece of watermelon rind, transferred its evil potency to the body of the little beast that ate it. But it was sport to hang him up as I had seen the men do at the ranch when butchering a sheep, to skin him and dress the meat, and pretend it was a stew for Isabel, the doll. I had a large collection of squirrel skins tacked up on the barn at the Shepherd house.

After a couple of years we built our own house in the same neighborhood on the south-east corner of Court and Hill Streets. It began as a seven room cottage, white with green blinds to suit father. Later the roof was raised and a second story inserted and the house painted a more fashionable all-over gray, to suit the ladies.

My mother was a happy woman when, after eleven years of married life, she moved into her very own home. A few months later she suddenly died, leaving my father widowed a second time, a lonely man for the remaining fourteen years of his life.

Mother had never been a strong woman and was unable to withstand an attack of typhus fever, contracted when on an errand of kindliness to a sick and forlorn seamstress. I often wish I might have an adult's knowledge of mother,—my child memories are beautiful. She was tall and slender, with quantities of heavy brown hair, dark eyes, and unusual richness of color in her cheeks which is repeated in some of her grandchildren. It amuses me to recall that I had such absolute faith in her word that on one occasion when she had visited my school and a girl remarked upon what a beautiful mother I had, I stoutly denied the allegation, for had she not herself assured me that she was not pretty?

I suppose that her New England conscience and native modesty could not allow even her little daughter to tell her how lovely she really was. I am told that she "had a knack of clothes" and I remember some of them well enough to confirm the opinion. Her taste allowed beautiful materials and much real lace, but of jewels there were none except some brooches that performed useful service and the wedding and engagement rings that held sentiment.

It was a sad thing that just when her dearest wish, that for her own home, was fulfilled, she must leave it and her three babies for some one else to care for. Fortunately her dearly loved, next-older sister was able to take her place.

At the time we built there seemed to be but two styles of architecture in vogue, one square on a four room base and the other oblong on a six room plan, the narrow end being to the street, with one tier of rooms shoved back a little in order to provide a small porch—we chose the latter. Every such house had a bay window in the projecting end, that being the front parlor, and all windows visible from the street must have yellow, varnished inside blinds.

One evening while the building was going on we went over as usual for our daily inspection and noted that the newly set studding marked the coming rooms. The connecting parlors seemed small to our eyes and tastes not yet trained to apartment and bungalow court proportions, so on the following morning father ordered out the wall between proposed front and back parlor, and our large sitting room,—living room it would be called today,—was ordained. it was unusual in Los Angeles where the prevailing mode demanded the two parlors. This room was large enough, 18′×33′, to stand the height of the ceiling, fourteen feet. Wide, high double-doors opened into the hall, opposite similar ones into the reception room, giving a feeling of spaciousness to the house.

The furnishing was of necessity more or less that which it is now customary to damn as mid-Victorian,—walnut furniture and a wealth of varying design in carpet, curtains, upholstery, wall-paper; but the whole in this case was kept in harmony by a key color, a medium olive, relieved by soft shades of rose and tan. Even the woodwork was painted to match the ground color of the walls, instead of glistening in the usual glory of varnished redwood or yellow pine. Everything was in good taste except a fearful and wonderful ceiling that was wished on us by the local wallpapering nabob. How fortunate that the walls were so high it was almost out of sight!

Over our heads were the two plaster of Paris centerpieces from which lighting fixtures sprang, first hanging lamps with prismatic fringes, later gas chandeliers. These fruits and flowers were tinted and gilded. Around them was a cream colored sky, set with golden stars, small ones, not planets,—limited in extent by an oval band of brocaded red velvet, this being the pet aversion of Aunt Martha. Outside this pale there was a field of metallic colored paper with an all-over design like chicken wire; next came a border of flowers and something modest to connect the whole artistic creation with the side wall.

We had a ceiling, but there were many things characteristic of the period that we did not have. We never had a "throw," nor a gilded milking stool with a ribbon bow on one leg; we never had a landscape painted on the stem of a palm leaf, nor oranges on a section of orange wood; we did not hang in any door a portière made of beads, shells, chenille ropes or eucalyptus seeds, all of which things were abroad in the land.

The room contained four bookcases, a rosewood square piano, a large table, a sofa and several easy chairs. From the walls looked down upon us Pharoah's Horses, The Stag in the Glen, and the Drove at the Ford, (suitable subjects the vogue provided for a family dependent upon livestock), but these were not all, for there were a few reproductions of old masters, a fine portrait of grandfather in his youth, and a picture of the sweet-faced mother who had gone to Heaven, as we children said.

At one end of the room was a white marble mantel with a large grate, always annoying us by its white patchiness in the low toned room, but contributing cheer with the coal fire that, through more than half the year, burned all day long. Los Angeles had no furnaces in those days, but the family was suited by the single fireplace, for one could choose the climate he wished from torrid zone near the grate to arctic in the bay window, where the goldfish circled their watery globe.

The room was the center of a happy family life, where, of an evening, all read by the light of the student lamp, or indulged in games, dominoes, authors, crambo, or logomachy, sugar-coated ways of getting training respectively in addition, names of books and writers, verse-making and spelling. Father rarely went out, and after the reading of his evening paper might join a lively domino tournament or amuse himself with solitaire.

Until the very last years of his life he busied himself at odd jobs about the house. Sometimes it would be a session with the grandfather clock, sometimes it would be chopping wood. He had the willow brought up from the ranch in long pieces, which he cut and stacked under the house. He raised chickens and at first cared for a horse and cow. Later we kept two horses, dispensed with the cow, and had a man for the livestock and garden and to drive us about town. We did not have a dog regularly but always cats, classical cats. Æneas was very long-legged and Dido lived with us a long time. I think it was she who went every evening with father for his after dinner walk and cigar.

One Thanksgiving time the wagon from the ranch came, bringing us a couple of barrels of apples, a load of wood and a fine turkey for the feast day. Imagine our dismay, one afternoon, to see it mount up on its wings and soar majestically from our hill top backyard down to the corner of first and Broadway below. He escaped us but, I presume, to some one else he came as a direct answer to prayer.

Father was always interested in flowers and was very successful in making them grow. Usually there was a box of slips out in the back yard. Often he would bring in a rich red Ragged Robin bud, dew-wet, to lay by mother's napkin for breakfast. For himself he put a sprig of lemon-verbena in his button-hole. For some reason, he excepted orange colored flowers from his favor. He made mock of the gay little runners by twisting their name into "nasty-urchins."

The windows of my room, directly over the parlor, were covered with a large, climbing "Baltimore Belle," an old-fashioned small cluster rose that I never see now-a-days. From my side window I looked out on a long row of blue-blossomed agapanthus, interspersed with pink belladonnas, flowers that in summer repeated the blue of the mountains touched at sunset with pink lights.

Every night when ready for bed, I opened the inside blinds and looked at the mountains and up to the stars and enlarged my heart, for what can give one the sense of awe and beauty that the night sky does?

The location of our home on the brow of a hill was chosen because of the view and the sense of air and space. Below us was the little city, the few business blocks, the homes set in gardens on tree shaded streets, the whole surrounded by orchards and vineyards. On clear days we could see the mountains far in the east and the ocean at San Pedro, with Santa Catalina beyond.

One very rainy winter, possible '86, we watched the flood waters from the river creep up Aliso Street and into Alameda: we saw bridges go out and small houses float down stream. Then it was that Martin Aguierre, a young policeman, won the admiration of everyone when he rode his black horse into the torrent and rescued flood victims from floating houses and debris in mid-stream. One of the girls in my room at school lost all her clothing except what she wore, and we had a "drive" for our local flood-sufferer.

This was a very different river in summer. I once saw a woman whose nerves had been wracked by dangerous winter fordings when the water swirled about the body of the buggy, get out of her carriage, letting it ford the Los Angeles river while she stepped easily across the entire stream. She had a complex, but she didn't know that name for her fear!

Beyond the river and up the hill on the other side stood, stark and lonely, the "Poor House," the first unit of the present County Hospital. Many a time when the skies forbore to rain I had it pointed out to me as my probable ultimate destination; for, after the bad middle years of the seventies when to a general financial depression was added a pestilence that killed off all the lambs, and to that was added a disastrous investment in mines, the firm of Flint, Bixby & Co. was sadly shaken, and it was of great moment whether or not sufficient moisture should come to provide grass and grain for the stock. So, if the sun shone too constantly and the year wore on to Christmas without a storm the ominous words, "a dry year," were heard and the bare building across the river loomed menacingly. But it always rained in time to save us!

Rain and overflowing rivers connote mud. Walkers on the cement sidewalks beside our paved streets little realize what wonderful mud was lost when Progress covered our adobe. With its first wetting it became very slippery on top of a hard base, but as more water fell and it was kneaded by feet and wheels, it became first like well-chewed gum and then a black porridge. I have seen signs that warned against drowning in the bog in the business center of town. An inverted pair of boots sticking out of a pile of mud in front of the old Court House once suggested that a citizen had gone in head first and disappeared.

Small boys turned an honest nickel or two by providing plank foot-bridges or selling individual "crickets" which the wayfarer might take with him from corner to corner. As the sun came out and the mud thickened the streets became like monstrous strips of sticky fly paper. We walked the cobblestone gutters until our rubbers were in shreds, or, when necessity drove us into the gum, lost them.

A friend assures me that one Sunday morning she set out for a church near the center of the city, that she made slow progress for a block and a half, and then, realizing that so much time had passed that she could not arrive in time for service, turned around and went home. It had taken her an hour and a half to make the round trip amounting to three blocks.

There is no mud so powerful when it is in its prime as adobe, and when it dries in all its trampled ridges and hollows, it is as hard as a rock. It takes all summer to wear it down level, ready to begin over again with the new rains. There are a few places yet, where, some rainy day if you are feeling extra fit, you may try to sympathize with a captured fly.

Certain other interesting kinds of soil are also covered up in Los Angeles. On the southwest corner of Temple and Broadway there is mica cropping out between the strata, and up by Court Street Angel's Flight there is a nice white formation very like chalk. I liked to cut it into odd shapes.

1926

TOM CLARK

Things to Do in California (1980)

Play beach volleyball
Make surfboards & live at Dana Pt.
Pick up chicks galore
Shine it on & get a good suntan
Catch cancer from the chemicals in the water
Die a grotesque death
Have a movie made about your life
Make sure you look thin in every scene

Priests of Newport, Manhattan & Laguna

The soi-distant "arrested and/or automated
adolescent," a market analyst unmarked by 29 autumns,
goes to the wet bar in his Baal Beach condominium
and blends a potent combination
of limeade, rum and ice cold yogurt

"Time to get happy," he tells us,
as he gets ready to go out into the Babylonian noon
& kick sand in somebody's face
with a foot that's a nearly perfect prosthesis
from suntanned tendons to golden fat of calf

The lost hard "g" in Los Angeles

The lost hard "g" in Los Angeles
a consonantal position swept away like all else
in the great laissez faire flood
from Chula Vista to Los Olivos
Jack Webb said it as
"Los Ang-less"

So did my grandfather, who liked it here

Nowadays though, they say it soft
without much meaning
to change it, but changing it
all the same—like taking the "O"
out of "Adios," and putting it back in "Idiot"

Or like the big developer in tartan plaids
who says to the local don of Zoning
Buon giorno! on a beautiful morning
before they divvy up the rights to the aqua
for another patch of the sun-deluged townhouses
that stretch from her to Solvang
in an unraveling irregular torus like an orange
peeled by an unsteady celestial hand

In a Vacuum, a Single Emission Can Become Smog

This part of the country is definitely a
corner pocket when it comes to word
music. For instance although he's
got a tin ear over there under the palm
trees and Nazi architecture of Cal Tech
the only poet/editor in SoCal who can fit
an entire cantaloupe in his mouth
without opening his lips
is being interviewed by the L.A. Times
as a force in the Arts
because of his new magazine named after farts
featuring the works of Mr. Dull and Mr. Slack,
snores in front and snoozes in the back.

The L.A. Times makes sure
to get all this straight so tomorrow
morning out there under the rat cluttered palm trees
of Nowhere, the suckers & hustlers & dilettantes
can lap it up. And when they do,
it will thereby become The Culture.

1980

EDUARDO GALEANO

The Winner

1931: Hanwell

CHARLIE THE Tramp visits Hanwell School. He walks on one leg, as if skating. He twists his ear and out spurts a stream of water. Hundreds of children orphaned, poor, or abandoned, scream with laughter. Thirty-five years ago, Charlie Chaplin was one of these children. Now he recognizes the chair he used to sit on and the corner of the dismal gym where he was birched.

Later he had escaped to London. In those days, shop windows displayed sizzling pork chops and golden potatoes steeped in gravy; Chaplin's nose still remembers the smell that filtered through the glass to mock him. And still engraved in his memory are the prices of other unattainable treats: a cup of tea, one halfpenny; a bit of herring, one penny; a tart, twopence.

Twenty years ago he left England in a cattle boat. Now he returns, the most famous man in the world. A cloud of journalists follows him like his shadow, and wherever he goes crowds jostle to see him, touch him. He can do whatever he wants. At the height of the talkie euphoria, his silent films have a devastating success. And he can spend whatever he wants—although he never wants. On the screen, Charlie the Tramp, poor leaf in the wind, knows nothing of money; in reality, Charles Chaplin, who perspires millions, watches his pennies and is incapable of looking at a painting without calculating its price. He will never share the fate of Buster Keaton, a man with open pockets, from whom everything flies away as soon as he earns it.

The Loser

1932: Hollywood

BUSTER KEATON arrives at the Metro studios hours late, dragging the hangover of the last night's drinking spree: feverish eyes, coppery tongue, dishrag muscles. Who knows how he manages to execute the clownish pirouettes and recite the idiotic jokes ordered by the script.

Now his films are talkies and Keaton is not allowed to improvise; nor may he do retakes in search of that elusive instant when poetry discovers imprisoned laughter and unchains it. Keaton, genius of liberty and silence, must follow to the letter the charlatan scenarios written by others. In this way costs are halved and talent eliminated, according to the production norms of the movie factories of the sound-film era. Left behind forever are the days when Hollywood was a mad adventure.

Every day Keaton feels more at home with dogs and cows. Every night he opens a bottle of bourbon and implores his own memory to drink and be still.

Brecht

1942: Hollywood

HOLLYWOOD manufactures films to turn the frightful vigil of humanity, on the point of annihilation, into sweet dreams. Bertolt Brecht, exiled from Hitler's Germany, is employed in this sleeping-pill industry. Founder of a theater that sought to open eyes wide, he earns his living at the United Artists studio, just one more writer who works office hours for Hollywood, competing to produce the biggest daily ration of idiocies.

On one of these days, Brecht buys a little God of Luck for forty cents in a Chinese store and puts it on his desk. Brecht has been told that the God of Luck licks his lips each time they make him take poison.

Carmen Miranda

1946: Hollywood

SEQUINED AND dripping with necklaces, crowned by a tower of bananas, Carmen Miranda undulates against a cardboard tropical backdrop.

Born in Portugal, daughter of a penurious barber who crossed the ocean, Carmen is the chief export of Brazil. Next comes coffee.

This diminutive hussy has little voice, and what she has is out of tune, but she sings with her hands and with her gleaming eyes, and that is more than enough. She is one of the best-paid performers in Hollywood. She has ten houses and eight oil wells.

But Fox refuses to renew her contract. Senator Joseph McCarthy has called her obscene, because at the peak of one of her production numbers, a photographer revealed intolerable glimpses of bare flesh and who knows what else under her flying skirt. And the press has disclosed that in her tenderest infancy Carmen recited lines before King Albert in Belgium, accompanying them with wiggles and winks that scandalized the nuns and gave the king prolonged insomnia.

Rita

1950: Hollywood

CHANGING HER name, weight, age, voice, lips, and eyebrows, she conquered Hollywood. Her hair was transformed from dull black into flaming red. To broaden her brow, they removed hair after hair by painful electrolysis. Over her eyes they put lashes like petals.

Rita Hayworth disguised herself as a goddess, and perhaps was one—for the forties, anyway. Now, the fifties demand something new.

Marilyn

1950: Hollywood

LIKE RITA, this girl has been improved. She had thick eyelashes and a double chin, a nose round at the tip, and large teeth. Hollywood reduced the fat, suppressed the cartilage, filed the teeth, and turned the mousy chestnut hair into a cascade of gleaming gold. Then the technicians baptized her Marilyn Monroe and invented a pathetic childhood story for her to tell the journalists.

This new Venus manufactured in Hollywood no longer needs to climb into strange beds seeking contracts for second-rate roles in third-rate films. She no longer lives on hot dogs and coffee, or suffers the cold of winter. Now she is a star; or rather a small personage in a mask who would like to remember, but cannot, that moment when she simply wanted to be saved from loneliness.

1988

CHARLES BUKOWSKI

Hollywood

S O , T H E R E I was over 65 years old, looking for my first house. I remembered how my father had virtually mortgaged his whole life to buy a house. He had told me, "Look, I'll pay for one house in my lifetime and when I die you'll get that house and then in your lifetime you'll pay for a house and when you die you'll leave those houses to your son. That'll make two houses. Then your son will . . . "

The whole process seemed terribly slow to me: house by house, death by death. Ten generations, ten houses. Then it would take just one person to gamble all those houses away, or burn them down with a match and then run down the street with his balls in a fruit-picker's pail.

Now I was looking for a house I really didn't want and I was going to write a screenplay I really didn't want to write. I was beginning to lose control and I realized it but I seemed unable to reverse the process.

The first realtor we stopped at was in Santa Monica. it was called TwentySecond Century Housing. Now, that was modern.

Sarah and I got out of the car and walked in. There was a young fellow at the desk, bow tie, nice striped shirt, red suspenders. He looked hip. He was shuffling papers at his desk. He stopped and looked up.

"Can I help you?"

"We want to buy a house," I said.

The young fellow just turned his head to one side and kept looking away. A minute went past. Two minutes.

"Let's go," I said to Sarah.

We got back into the car and I started the engine.

"What was all that about?" Sarah asked.

"He didn't want to do business with us. He took a reading and he thought we were indigent, worthless. He thought we would waste his time."

"But it's not true."

"Maybe not, but the whole thing made me feel as if I was covered with slime."

I drove the car along, hardly knowing where I was going.

Somehow, that had hurt. Of course, I was hungover and I needed a shave and I always wore clothing that somehow didn't seem to fit me quite right and maybe all the years of poverty had just given me a certain look. But I didn't think it was wise to judge a man from the outside like that. I would much rather judge a man on the way he acted and spoke.

"Christ," I laughed, "maybe nobody will sell us a house!"

"The man was a fool," said Sarah.

"TwentySecond Century Housing is one of the largest real estate chains in the state."

"The man was a fool," Sarah repeated.

I still felt diminished. Maybe I *was* a jerk-off of some kind. All I knew how to do was to type—sometimes.

Then we were in a hilly area driving along.

"Where are we?" I asked.

"Topanga Canyon," Sarah answered.

"This place looks fucked."

"It's all right except for floods and fires and burned-out-neohippy types."

Then I saw the sign: APES HAVEN. It was a bar. I pulled up alongside and we got out. There was a cluster of bikes outside. Sometimes called hogs.

We went in. It was damn near full. Fellows in leather jackets. Fellows wearing dirty scarfs. Some of the fellows had scabs on their faces. Others had beards that didn't grow quite right. Most of the eyes were pale blue and round and listless. They sat very still as if they had been there for weeks.

We found a couple of stools.

"Two beers," I said, "anything in a bottle."

The barkeep trotted off.

The beers came back and Sarah and I had a hit.

Then I noticed a face thrust forward along the bar looking at us. It was a very fat round face, a touch imbecilic. It was a young man and his hair and his beard were a dirty red, but his eyebrows were pure white. His lower lip hung down as if an invisible weight were pulling at it, the lip was twisted and you saw the inner lip and it was set and it shimmered.

"Chinaski," he said, "son of a bitch, it's CHINASKI!"

I gave a small wave, then looked straight ahead.

"One of my readers," I said to Sarah.

"Oh oh," she said.

"Chinaski," I heard a voice to my right.

"Chinaski," I heard another voice.

A whiskey appeared before me. I lifted it, "Thank you, fellows!" and I knocked it off.

"Go easy," said Sarah, "you know how you are. We'll never get out of here."

The bartender brought another whiskey. He was a little guy with dark red blotches all over his face. He looked meaner than anybody in there. He just stood there, staring at me.

"Chinaski," he said, "the world's greatest writer."

"If you insist," I said and raised the glass of whiskey. Then I passed it to Sarah who knocked it off.

She gave a little cough and set the glass down.

"I only drank that to help save you."

Then there was a little group gathering slowly behind us.

"Chinaski. Chinaski . . . Motherfuck . . . I've read all your books, ALL YOUR BOOKS! . . . I can kick your ass, Chinaski . . . Hey, Chinaski, can you still get it up? . . . Chinaski, Chinaski, can I read you one of my poems?"

I paid the barkeep and we backed off our stools and moved toward the door. Again I noticed the leather jackets and the blandness of the faces and the feeling that there wasn't much joy or daring in any of them. There was something totally missing in the poor fellows and something in me wrenched, for just a moment, and I felt like throwing my arms around them, consoling and embracing them like some Dostoyevsky, but I knew that would finally lead nowhere except to ridicule and humiliation, for myself and for them. The world had somehow gone too far, and spontaneous kindness could never be so easy. It was something we would all have to work for once again.

And they followed us out. "Chinaski, Chinaski . . . Who's your beautiful lady? You don't deserve her, man! . . . Chinaski, come on, stay and drink with us! Be a good guy! Be like your writing, Chinaski! Don't be a prick!"

They were right, of course. We got in the car and I started the engine and we drove slowly through them as they crowded around us, slowly giving way, some of them blowing kisses, some of them giving me the finger, a few beating on the windows. We got through.

We made it to the road and drove along.

"So," said Sarah, "those are your readers?"

"That's most of them, I think."

"Don't any intelligent people read you?"

"I hope so."

We kept driving along not saying anything. Then Sarah asked, "What are you thinking about?"

"Dennis Body."

"Dennis Body? What's that?"

"He was my only friend in grammar school. I wonder whatever happened to him."

As we drove along, I saw it: Rainbow Realty.

I pulled up in front. The parking area was not paved and there were large potholes and ruts everywhere. I located the flattest surface, then parked. We got out and walked to the office. The door was open and a fat dirty white chicken sat there. I nudged it with my foot. It stood up, emitted a bit of matter and walked into the office, found a place in the corner and sat down again.

There was a lady at the desk, mid-forties, thin, with straight mud-colored hair embossed with a paper flower, red. She was drinking a beer and smoking a Pall Mall.

"Shit, howdy!" she greeted us, "looking for a place, roundabouts?"

"You might say," I answered.

"Well, *say* it then! Ha, ha, ha!"

She knocked her beer off, handed me a card.

```
┌─────────────────────────────────────┐
│          RAINBOW REALTY              │
│        Indeed, I got what you        │
│                need.                 │
│                                      │
│                                      │
│             Lila Grant,              │
│           at your service            │
└─────────────────────────────────────┘
```

Lila stood up.

"Follow me . . . "

She didn't lock the office. She got into her car. It was a '62 Comet. I knew because I once had a '62 Comet. In fact, it looked like the same one I had sold for junk.

We followed her up a rural winding dirt road. We drove for some minutes. I noted the absence of street lights. Also, on each side of the road were deep canyons. I made a note that driving along there at night with a few drinks in you could be hazardous.

Finally, we pulled up in front of an unpainted wooden house. Well, it had been painted, once, a long time ago but the weather had worn away almost all the paint that had been a henshit white to begin with. The house seemed to sag forward and to the left—our left, as we got out of the car. It was a big house, looked homey, earthy.

All of this, I thought, because I've accepted an advance to write a screenplay and because I've got a tax consultant.

We walked up on the porch and the boards, of course, sagged under our weight. I scaled in at 228, most of it fat instead of muscle. My fighting days were over. To think I had once weighed 144 pounds on a 6-foot frame: the grand old starving days when I was writing the good stuff.

Lila beat on the front door.

"Darlene, honey? You decent? You better be because our butts are a-comin' in! Got some folks who wanna see your castle! Ha, ha, ha!"

Lila pushed the door open and we walked in.

It was dark inside and it smelled like there was a turkey burning in the oven. Also, there was the feeling of shadowy winged creatures floating about. A light bulb hung down from a cord. The insulation had peeled away and you could see the bare wire. I felt something like a cold wind at the back of my neck. Then I realized it was only a rush of fear. I shook that idea off with the thought, this place has got to be really cheap.

Then Darlene emerged from the darkness. Big lipstick mouth. Hair in all directions. Eyes gushing kindness to cover up years of waste. She was fat in blue jeans and faded flower blouse. Two earrings like eyeballs, they hung there swinging a bit, those blue irises. She was holding a rolled joint. She rushed forward.

"Lila, you chippy! What's hangin'?"

Lila took the joint from Darlene's hand, took a drag, handed it back.

"How's your ol' peg-legged-fool-of-a-brother, Willy?"

"Oh, shit, he just got thrown in county jail. He's scared shitless they're gonna get him in the ass!"

"Don't worry, honey, he's too hog-ugly."

"You really think so?"

"Really."

"I hope so!"

Then we were introduced around. Then there was silence. We stood there as if we had lost all power of thought, of what we were about. I rather liked it. I thought, well, this is all right, I can stand around here as long as anybody. I concentrated on the twisted wire of the light bulb cord.

A tall thin man slowly entered. He walked toward us, one stiff leg at a time. He put one leg forward and then deliberately followed it with the other. He was like a blind man without a cane. He came toward us. His face was a mass of beard and the thick hair was twisted, tangled. But he had beautiful eyes, a dark dark green. Emeralds for eyes. The sucker was worth something. And he had a *big smile*. He walked closer. Stopped and kept *smiling, smiling*.

"This is my husband," said Darlene, "this is Double Quartet."

He nodded. Sarah and I nodded back.

Lila leaned toward me, whispered, "They both usta be in the movie business."

Sarah was getting tired of the time all this took.

"Well, let's have a look at the place!"

"Why, *sure,* honey, you all bring your ass and folla me . . . "

We followed Lila into the other room and as we did I glanced back. I saw Double Quartet take the joint from Darlene and have a drag.

Jesus, he had such great eyes; eyes are truly the reflection of the soul. But, damn, that *big big smile* ruined it all.

We were evidently in the dining room or the front room. There was no furniture. There was an empty water bed nailed to one of the walls and across the water bed, scrawled in red paint was:

THE SPIDER SINGS ALONE

"Looka this," Lila said, "look at that yard. Some nice *land!*"

We looked out of the window. The yard was like the road, only more so: large potholes, neglected mounds of dirt and rock. And out there, sitting all by itself, upright, was a lone, discarded toilet. The lid was missing.

"That's nice," I said, "kind of odd."

"These here people are ARTISTS," said our realtor.

We stepped back. I touched the curtain that covered the window. Where I touched it a piece of the curtain dropped away.

"These here people are *deep* inside," said Lila. "They just don't bother with the *ordinaries,* you know."

We went upstairs and the stairway was solid, strangely so. It was good and true, and I felt a little better then, walking up there.

All that there was in the bedroom was a water bed but this one was full. It sat in the far corner, lonely by itself. One strange thing, there was a large swelling at one edge. It gave the impression of an explosion to come.

The bathroom was tiled but the floor had gone unwashed for so long that the tiles had almost disappeared in the smear of dirt and footprints.

The toilet was brown-crusted, forever. No ever changing that. There was crust upon crust upon crust. It was worse than any toilet I had ever seen in any dive, in any bar I had ever been in, and I began to gag at the memory of all those crappers and at the thought of this one here. I walked out for a moment, steadied myself, inhaled, made up my mind not to think about any of it, and then re-entered the bathroom.

"Sorry," I said.

Lila understood. "Shit, pard," she said. "It's all right . . . "

I didn't look *in* the bathtub but did note that somebody had scrawled with various colored paints on the wall over the bathtub:

IF TIM LEARY AIN'T GOD,
THEN GOD IS DEAD.

MY FATHER DIED IN THE
ABRAHAM LINCOLN BRIGADE
AND THE DEVIL HAS A
PUSSY

CHARLES LINDBERG WAS
A
COCKSUCKER

There were a few other messages painted here and there but they were smeared and garbled and difficult to read.

"I'm gonna let you two wander about, you know, so you can get the feel. Buying a home is a real head-shaker. I don't want to rush you none."

Then Lila left. We heard her going down the stairway. Sarah and I stepped out into the hallway. Hanging near us, from a frayed rope, was an old rusted coffeepot.

"Oh my god," Sarah said suddenly, "my god!"

"What is it?"

"I've seen photos of this house before! I remember now! I *thought* it looked familiar!"

"What? What is it?"

"This is one of the houses where *Charles Manson* killed somebody!"

"Are you sure?"

"Yes, yes!"

"Let's get out of here . . . "

We went on down the stairway. They were waiting for us down there: Lila, Darlene and Double Quartet.

"Well," asked Lila, "what do you think?"

"I've got your card with your phone number," I told her. "We can get in touch."

"If you people are artists," said Darlene, "we can knock some off the price. We like artists. Are you artists?"

"No," I said. "Well, I'm not, anyhow."

"I can show you some more places," said Lila.

"No, no," said Sarah, "we've seen enough today. We have to rest up."

We had to push past them, and all the time Double Quartet just kept *smiling, smiling . . .*

The place I was living in at that time did have some qualities. One of the finest was the bedroom which was painted a dark, dark blue. That dark dark blue had provided a haven for many a hangover, some of them brutal enough to almost kill a man, especially at a time when I was popping pills which people would give me without my bothering to ask what they were. Some nights I knew that if I slept I would die. I would walk around alone all night, from the bedroom to the bathroom and from the bathroom through the front room and into the kitchen. I opened and closed the refrigerator, time and time again. I turned the faucets on and off. Then I went to the bathroom and turned the faucets on and off. I flushed the toilet. I pulled at my ears. I inhaled and exhaled. Then, when the sun came up, I knew I was safe. Then I would sleep with the dark dark blue walls, healing.

Another feature of that place were the knocks of unsavory women at 3 or 4 a.m. They certainly weren't ladies of great charm, but having a foolish turn of mind, I felt that somehow they brought me adventure. The real fact of the matter was that many of them had no place else to go. And they liked the fact that there was drink and that I didn't work too hard trying to bed down with them.

Of course, after I met Sarah, this part of my lifestyle changed quite a bit.

That neighborhood around Carlton Way near Western Avenue was changing too. It had been almost all lower-class white, but political troubles in Central America and other parts of the world had brought a new type of individual to the neighborhood. The male usually was small, a dark or light brown, usually young. There were wives, children, brothers, cousins, friends. They began filling up the apartments and courts. They lived many to an apartment and I was one of the few whites left in the court complex.

The children ran up and down, up and down the court walkway. They all seemed to be between two and seven years old. They had no bikes or toys. The wives were seldom seen. They remained inside, hidden. Many of the men also remained inside. It was not wise to let the landlord know how many people were living in a single unit. The few men seen outside were the legal renters. At least they paid the rent. How they survived was unknown. The men were small, thin, silent, unsmiling. Most sat on the porch steps in their undershirts, slumped forward a bit, occasionally smoking a cigarette. They sat on the porch steps for hours, motionless. Sometimes they purchased very old junk automobiles and the men drove them *slowly* around the neighborhood. They had no auto insurance or driver's licenses and they drove with expired license plates. Most of the cars had defective brakes. The men almost never stopped at the corner stop sign and often failed to heed red lights, but there were few accidents. Something was watching over them.

After a while the cars would break down but my new neighbors wouldn't leave them on the street. They would drive them up the walkways and park them directly outside their door. First they would work on the engine. They would take off the hood and the engine would rust in the rain. Then they would put the car on blocks and remove the wheels. They took the wheels inside and kept them there so they wouldn't be stolen at night.

While I was living there, there were two rows of cars lined up in the court, just sitting there on blocks. The men sat motionless on their porches in their undershirts. Sometimes I would nod or wave to them. They never responded. Apparently they couldn't understand or read the eviction notices and they tore them up, but I did see them studying the daily L.A. papers. They were stoic and durable because compared to where they had come from, things were now easy.

Well, no matter. My tax consultant had suggested I purchase a house, and so for me it wasn't really a matter of "white flight." Although, who knows? I had noticed that each time I had moved in Los Angeles over the years, each move had always been to the North and to the West.

Finally, after a few weeks of house hunting, we found the one. After the down payment the monthly payments came to $789.81. There was a huge hedge in front on the street and the yard was also in front so the house sat way back on the lot. It looked like a damned good place to hide. There was even a stairway, an *upstairs* with a bedroom, bathroom and what was to become by typing room. And there was an old desk left in there, a huge ugly old thing. Now, after decades, I was a writer with a desk. Yes, I felt the fear, the fear of becoming like *them*. Worse, I had an assignment to write a screenplay. Was I doomed and damned, was I about to be sucked dry? I didn't feel it would be that way. But does anybody, ever?

Sarah and I moved our few possessions in.

The big moment came. I sat the typewriter down on the desk and I put a piece of paper in there and I hit the keys. The typewriter still worked. And there was plenty of room for an ashtray, the radio and the bottle. Don't let anybody tell you different. Life begins at 65.

1989

Author Biographies

F. SCOTT FITZGERALD, the suave, best-selling author of *The Great Gatsby* and *Tender Is the Night,* moved to Hollywood to pen what many thought would be the classic Hollywood novel, *The Last Tycoon.* He worked on that never-to-be-finished tome as well as the short story "Crazy Sunday" in 1940, the last year of his life.

L.A. native KATE BRAVERMAN's tropical *Palm Latitudes* is her first novel.

OSCAR ZETA ACOSTA, the legendary Robin Hood-like Chicano lawyer, mysteriously disappeared in 1971. His leadership in the militant Chicano movement of the late '6os, as well as his routinely insane antics, made him the model for Hunter S. Thompson's "Dr. Gonzo."

Pulitzer Prize–winning playwright SAM SHEPARD recalled his childhood memories of growing up in Pasadena and outer Los Angeles in *Motel Chronicles,* which was later to be used as the basis for the film *Paris, Texas.*

JOHN FANTE's best-known novels and screenplays, such as *Full of Life* and *Walk on the Wild Side,* were set in hardboiled 1940s L.A. *Ask the Dust* was his second novel, written in 1938.

HELEN HUNT JACKSON's *Ramona* is the classic novel of society life in nineteenth-century Los Angeles.

NATHANAEL WEST's *Day of the Locust* is widely considered to be the best novel ever written about Los Angeles. He died nearly unknown in 1940.

Actor JACK WEBB immortalized Joe Friday in TV's "Dragnet" and later penned a sort of book version of the series, *The Badge.*

RAYMOND CHANDLER, author of the classics *Lady in the Lake*

and *The Big Sleep*, worked in Hollywood and seems to have hated it. He told why in a 1945 issue of *The Atlantic*.

In 1949, CHARLES BRACKETT, BILLY WILDER and D. M. MARSHMAN, JR., collaborated on the ultimate Hollywood film, *Sunset Boulevard*, starring William Holden, Gloria Swanson and Erich Von Stroheim.

British wag MARTIN AMIS pens reeling novels like *Money, Success* and *London Fields*. On occasion, his books take him as far afield as Southern California, with amusing results.

HENRY MILLER drove across the United States in 1939, having just returned after ten years as an expatriate. *The Air-Conditioned Nightmare* is a log of truculent observations made while driving from New York all the way west to Hollywood, California.

SARAH BIXBY SMITH's memoirs of growing up in orange grove–laden Southern California are collected in her 1926 book, *Adobe Days*.

TOM CLARK's sweet and sour memories of life in the City of Angels are collected in *Paradise Resisted*, his 1980 book of western poems.

Uruguayan novelist EDUARDO GALEANO's trilogy, *Memory of Fire*, maps out, in brief vignettes, the entire history of the Americas. The selections on Los Angeles are from the third volume, *Century of the Wind*.

A native of Germany, CHARLES BUKOWSKI moved to L.A. when he was three and by his mid-twenties was chronicling the city's woolly underside in novels such as *Ham on Rye* and *Barfly*. *Hollywood* is his latest.

Credits

"Crazy Sunday" reprinted with permission of Charles Scribner's Sons, an imprint of Macmillan Publishing Company, from *The Short Stories of F. Scott Fitzgerald* by F. Scott Fitzgerald. Copyright 1931 by the Curtis Publishing Company, renewed 1959 by Frances Scott Fitzgerald Lanahan.

"Palm Latitudes" copyright 1988 by Kate Braverman. Reprinted by permission of Simon & Schuster, Inc.

"The Revolt of the Cockroach People" from *The Revolt of the Cockroach People* by Marcos Acosta. Copyright 1989 by Oscar Zeta Acosta. Reprinted by permission of Vintage Books, a division of Random House, Inc.

Poems by Sam Shepard from *Motel Chronicles,* copyright 1982 by Sam Shepard. Reprinted by permission of City Lights Books.

"Ask the Dust" from the novel *Ask the Dust* by John Fante, copyright 1939. Reprinted by permission of Black Sparrow Press.

The Day of the Locust, copyright 1939 by the Estate of Nathanael West, copyright 1966 by Laura Perlman.

"The Badge" by Jack Webb from *The Badge,* 1958. Reprinted by permission of Prentice-Hall.

"Writers in Hollywood" by Raymond Chandler originally appeared in *The Atlantic* in 1945. Reprinted with permission.

Excerpt from *Sunset Boulevard* copyright 1951 by Paramount Pictures Corporation. All rights reserved. Reprinted with permission.

"Money" from the novel *Money* by Martin Amis, copyright 1984. Reprinted by permission of Penguin Books.

"Soirée in Hollywood" from Henry Miller: *The Air-Conditioned Nightmare.* Copyright 1945 by New Directions Publishing Corporation.

Los Angeles Stories was designed by Herman + Company,
San Francisco, California. Cover design by John Miller.
Set in Perpetua by **T:H** Typecast Inc., Cotati, California.